The Romanian Incident

The Romanian Incident

A NOVEL

SIMON KING

Clearstream Books

An Imprint of Clearstream Entertainment

THE ROMANIAN INCIDENT. © 2022 by Simon King. All rights reserved. Printed in the United States of America. No part of this book may be used or reproduced in any manner whatsoever without written permission except in the case of brief quotations embodied in critical articles and reviews.

For information send email to: *simonkingwriter.com*

Copies of this book may be purchased for educational, business, or sales promotional use.

For information send email to: *simonkingwriter.com*

Cover design by RYVE Creative.

FIRST EDITION

Library of Congress Cataloging-in-Publication Data has been applied for.

ISBN: 978-1-7360634-0-8

10 9 8 7 6 5 4 3 2 1

*I am who I am because of a small group
of people who I love dearly.*

*This book is dedicated to my children:
Evan, Sean-Ryan, Dylan, Cheyenneh, and Diana.*

*A tender embrace is reserved for my darling wife
Elena, who keeps me focused, honest, and smiling.*

*But most of all, I dedicate this book to my
wonderful parents, Stan and Elsie.
Two more loving individuals have never
walked this earth. I would give anything to
have one more cup of tea with them.*

Prologue

It was unusual for Dan Steel to strike out with women, but twice in one evening was unheard of. He considered his first mark, Isabella Manson, to be a no-brainer. After all, he had taken her to bed on numerous occasions so tonight should have been no different. Granted, her anger over discovering she was no longer the movie star she believed herself to be, coupled with his state of inebriation, may have driven his chances into the ground. That said, Steel considered his chiseled good looks and way with words sufficient tools to make any woman overlook his love of the bottle.

The second failure came several hours later when he visited the hotel's opulent swimming pool in hopes of finding a late-night fling. The pounding in his head remained. He grabbed a bottle of vodka from his suitcase and two glasses from his room and headed downstairs. As he opened the double doors to the indoor pool area, he almost passed out as the poisonous odor of chlorine combined with the mixed drinks in his body. If not for the sight of a gloriously thin and gorgeously attractive young woman standing near the room's oversized windows, he would have given up on his quest immediately. Steel shook his head to clear the possibility of her being an apparition and then, steadying himself, strode purposely to where she stood. With each closing step he grew more and more desirous, but questions bounced between his ears. *Was she too young for him?* Nonsense! He never let a dramatic age difference stand between him and sex. *Was she alone?* An obstacle to be sure, but one he had overcome many times before.

"Bit late for a swim isn't it?" he said.

The woman, whose age did indeed seem to be a few multiples of ten less than his own, looked over her shoulder at Steel. She had wrapped her hair in a towel but drips of water as fine as a morning dew still glistened on her flawless skin.

"Are you lost?" she said, glancing quickly at his business suit.

"Lost? No. Oh, you mean the suit. It would seem I came to this hotel without knowing they had such a beautiful pool. I forgot my swim trunks."

"Pity."

Was this the invitation he needed? He held out the bottle and clinked the glasses against it.

"It appears you have finished your swim. Perhaps you will join me in a late-night drink?"

"Appears you've had a few already."

She thought for a moment before removing the towel from her head. Leaning forward, she massaged her hair with the towel in an attempt to squeeze even more water from the dark mass of tangled strands. The volume of hair on her head made this a trying task. Standing upright, she continued to vigorously dry her hair. Her body was a study in tone. Not a single ounce of fat or cellulite moved on her taught frame. The exceptions— which Dan Steel took great happiness in observing— were her breasts, which swayed gently from side-to-side in her tiny bikini.

Her hair sufficiently dry, she motioned to a nearby table.

"Come on then, let's have a little sip," she said.

This should have been the start of a fabulous evening, but the young woman had other ideas and they did not include rolling around in a hotel bed with some old American dude.

***

Dejected, Dan Steel left the pool area without the girl and without the bottle. Moments later, he entered his hotel room after struggling with the lock and failing to find the light switch inside. He stumbled over to a small desk and, with great effort, put his right foot on the accompanying chair to untie his shoe. Had he not been drunk, he may have taken the time to turn on the room's lights and discover he was not alone.

Chapter 1

The blizzard crashed through Romania's Făgăraş
Mountains with no direct or clear path. The frigid, frozen
terrain was broken only by the nauseating twists of the
Trans-Făgărașian highway. This passage was unpleasant
during the sunniest of times and any driver was sure to
stop once or twice to allow his green-faced passengers
respite to purge their stomachs. Today was not one of
those days.

Snow turned the few scattered trees into white
skeletons with only a hint of green left to indicate a forest
might exist on the mountain's steep slopes. As each tree
reached holding capacity, a blast of winter wind would

bend the branches toward the ground before snapping them back into shape and sending the snow off in an explosive white cloud of frozen water. The moon occasionally illuminated the stark whiteness of the hills, only to disappear once again behind the darkness of the storm. During these moments of almost complete nothingness, the distant lights of Teleki Castle shimmered; a welcome ray of civilization in an otherwise desolate world.

Teleki, as the locals called the structure, sat high on the hill where the highway straightened out for a few kilometers before dropping down the northern flank of the mountains. During the summer, the elegant hotel was a tourist destination, drawing visitors from as far away as communist Romania would allow. Once the winter cold started to chase the hikers and mushroom hunters back indoors, the owner shut down most of the hotel's rooms, leaving less than a dozen open for intrepid—or more likely, foolish—travelers who wished to escape the grayness and architectural redundancy of post-war Bucharest. While construction of the modern buildings in Romania's capitol followed the blocky style of Socialist realism and although the country no longer bowed to Stalinist leadership, the echoes of the not-so-distant past remained in the apartment blocks where the vast majority of Romanians lived.

Nicolae Ceausescu rose to power in the Romanian Communist Party less than a year earlier and he ruled in a fashion which often ran counter to the tightly-worded suggestions of Moscow. The country's citizens—many with the brutal wounds of Allied bombing raids still clearly etched in their memories— now experienced the iron fist of the up-and-coming politician's repressive government and learning to live in fear.

Other than the glimmer of glowing life offered by Teleki, an occasional flash of light danced along the highway far below the castle. A 1966 Mercedes Pagoda Roadster, fresh from the showrooms of Western Europe, tore up the road at breakneck speed, the automobile's bright red paint job in sharp contrast to the white mountains. Driving at summer speeds with little care for the weather, the car swerved hard to the right, left, and then right again, always managing to find enough traction to move forward up the treacherous highway. The evidence was clear: an expert driver, one trained in both taking on the challenges of a blizzard while pushing the sports car to proving-ground limits, was at the wheel.

Vast pillows of white lined the highway which was hidden under more than twenty centimeters of untracked white powder with more falling every minute. An occasional road sign was the only indication a path existed beneath the blizzard's blanket. Virgin snow flew wildly in either direction as the Mercedes raced up the highway, tires spinning, barely able to find traction. A pair of slender, black leather gloved hands manipulated the steering wheel with the learned skills of a Grand Prix racer, whipping the car back and forth in a search for the most secure path forward. The car's engine purred rather than strained, evidently enjoying the challenge the driver was putting the Mercedes through. With no hesitation, the driver's right hand descended from the steering wheel and wrapped around the polished gearshift, waiting for the precise moment to drop the car into a lower gear.

While the actions of the driver were calm and collected, the view out the windshield remained desperate as the wipers struggled against the storm and the Mercedes' headlights illuminated no more than ten meters of the road ahead. A new gear selected, the hand returned to the job of steering as the driver popped the clutch. The roadster lurched forward, leaving a deep path in the snow as the car passed a snow-plastered sign indicating TELEKI CASTLE - 1.5 KILOMETERS before disappearing into the distance. As this happened, snow spiraled into the air from the Mercedes' rear tires, creating a white tornado more complex than the blizzard itself. Within moments, the storm filled the car's tracks, returning the road to a virginal state.

One kilometer shy of the road's summit, a wall of granite rocks appeared on the right side of the highway. Built at a time when labor was cheap, the barrier reflected each curve and bump the Trans-Făgărașian had to offer. The blocks continued unbroken before eventually curving away from the road revealing a driveway of sorts. On either side of this drive, the wall rapidly rose up, creating two impressive columns. The lack of tracks provided proof no car had passed this way for hours. At the end of the private road sat Teleki, grander and even more intimidating than it had been from a distance. The castle's triple spires pierced skyward through the clouds, defying the storm and gravity. Despite the deep snow, the manicured grounds and expertly trimmed hedges, bushes, and trees were discernible.

No one would be faulted for describing Teleki as both classic and ancient. The hotel's style was clearly a remnant of early 1800s Romanian architecture. Like many similar structures in eastern Europe, the castle had fallen into disrepair in the years following the war, but with the growing interest in tourism and the money these visitors left in Romania, Teleki had undergone a full renovation and became one of the nation's primary selling points to the western world. In addition to being a monument to Romanian engineering, Teleki was now a hotel where the wealthy sipped fine wine and dined on local delicacies while ignoring the ravages of war communism had brought to the country over the years.

The hotel's efficient car park had been hand-shoveled to accommodate the few vehicles occupying spaces, but now those cars were no more than white mounds. If not for their location and alignment, they would be unrecognizable as automobiles. A substantial stone stairway climbed from the parking lot to the grand entrance of the resort and a not-immodest sign hanging above the oversized oak doors identified the structure as HOTEL TELEKI. Numerous windows on the main and second floors of the building emanated bright and warming light, inviting the lucky few who made the wintery drive to come inside for a sip of something warm.

Simon King

Chapter 2

"What to do?" Razvan said. "How am I to welcome guests if they cannot drive here? This storm…"

Razvan Petrescu's voice trailed off as he pulled heavily on his potent Gauloise. He stood at a full-length picture window outlined with floor-to-ceiling purple drapes. The window was one of pair on either side of the hotel lobby's oversized front doors. Razvan exhaled a dense cloud of gray smoke, which bounced off the glass and enveloped his face. Considering the hotel owner to be a pudgy man was a fair assessment as his sizable girth fell only shy of his diminutive height. He was in his mid-sixties and dressed in a pleasing light-brown suit and sporting a striped tie that matched his nation's red, yellow, and blue flag. Thinking him to be a politician or perhaps a university philosophy professor was not out of the question.

Razvan purchased the Teleki Castle from the Romanian government four years earlier. He paid what some described as pennies-on-the-dollar. The building and grounds were in utter disrepair when he brought in an army of international craftsmen to update the facility and turn the once decrepit structure into a beautiful resort hotel. Despite Romania's political distance from the wealthier nations to the west, Razvan had coaxed the nation's leaders to allow him to employ tile setters from Italy, landscape designers from France, and an interior designer from capitalist New York. He imported furniture manufactured in England and commissioned a photographer from Switzerland to produce images for the hotel's brochure. The hotel's crowning jewel was an indoor pool, which had become the envy of hotels and resorts throughout Europe. Of course, he had the opportunity to hire local workers to rebuild the castle, and they would have done excellent work, but Razvan wanted to announce to the world he had not scrimped a single Romanian leu to have the best. When speaking with anyone about the hotel, he leaned on his mother tongue rather than rely on his smattering of English and German. Besides, he believed his language to be far more beautiful and descriptive.

"Până ajungi la Dumnezeu, te mănâncă sfinţii," Razvan said in Romanian to no one in particular. Taking a last, long drag on his cigarette, he left his spot at the window and waddled effectively across the lobby toward the front desk.

"What did you say?" asked Crina Butaciu, the hotel's receptionist.

"My dear Crina," Razvan said in broken English, "we are in Romania. Be proud. Romanian is poetry to the ears while those other languages are a poor excuse for comic-book dialogue. You must learn to speak with the tongue of your parents and ancestors."

"Of course. I understand Romanian, Razvan, but I was unable to comprehend what you said as you sulked by the window."

"Before you reach God, the saints will eat you. This is what I said. Perhaps this is easier for you to grasp. You must not always rely on the bastard English language."

Crina was a beautiful woman by any standard. While she was approaching thirty, many believed her to be barely out of her teens. Today, as always, she wore a spotless and professionally-tailored black jacket and matching short skirt. The sheer pink blouse and minimal bra provided enough of a glimpse of her full breasts to attract the attention of the most chaste male guest. Though they brought her endless pain, Crina wore elegant heels which added several inches to her height. Nude-colored nylons accentuated every slight curve of her legs. While they were not visible inside her shoes, she'd painted her toenails to match the light-rose color on her fingernails which rested, perfectly manicured, at the end of her delicate hands. She preferred to have her long hair loose, and the auburn locks flowed gracefully with the slightest motion. Where Razvan was a bundle of nerves, confusion, and sometimes rudeness, Crina was kind, polite, precise, and tremendously knowledgeable.

Razvan crushed his cigarette into a spotlessly clean glass ashtray with more force than necessary. He examined his image in a mirror hanging near Crina's desk and straightened his tie for what must have been the hundredth time that evening. Grabbing some papers from the desk, Razvan thumbed through them without really giving the documents more than a cursory glance.

"How many are here? How many guests?" he asked. This was a question he bothered Crina with every day of the year.

"Razvan, don't worry. We're almost full." She realized the answer would not satisfy the ever-worried hotel owner. He would want details. "We have eight guests in seven rooms."

"No more? Only eight?"

"We have another guest reserved, but I'm not confident they will arrive given this storm."

This was an honest response, for when storms came to the mountains surrounding the hotel, sane people would certainly stay back in Bucharest or perhaps find a small inn or hostel in one of the larger villages between the city and the resort.

Razvan dropped the papers on the desk, making no attempt to keep them in a neat stack. He did this not out of spite, but because he believed a hotel owner must

14

always portray himself as being above trivialities, including being pleasant to his workers. Teleki employees each had a task, and he expected them to do these duties if they wished to remain in his employ. Privately, the workers had discussed this among themselves and frequently agreed something must be done and that Razvan must be told, but none of them was willing to put their job on the line to raise the topic with their employer.

"Please explain to me, how I am supposed to keep this hotel running with only seven guests? This cannot be done. This is impossible."

Crina sensed a lecture was soon to follow. Her boss was nothing if not predictable. As always, she smiled and carried on with her business rather than attempt to stop him or counter his arguments.

"Saying we are almost full is easy for you. You were crying in diapers when I was here trying to rebuild this place. From scratch, I rebuilt the horrid castle into a beautiful resort. With my bare hands and my own money. Five years. Five years, and no one. My savings went out the door and what do you suppose came in?"

This argument was not new to Crina; Razvan had gone on and on about the topic dozens of times before. She often awoke in the morning knowing with full certainty Razvan would rail on about concerns he had complained to her about only the day before. *Did he really expect anyone to think he had built the hotel on his own?* she thought.

"Wind," Crina said under her breath.

"I will tell you what, wind. Nothing else. No guests. And no money. Only wind."

Razvan pulled a well-fingered silver cigarette case from his jacket pocket. He removed a Gauloise, tapped the cigarette on the reception desk, and placed the razor-straight white tube between his lips while he secured a matching lighter from another pocket. The unlit cigarette bounced as he spoke. Crina was sure the Gauloise would break free of his plump lips at any moment and fall to the floor. The litter would remain at his feet until it was picked up by her because a man in his position did not clean floors despite the fact that he had created the mess.

"Is that any way to operate a hotel? I ask you, is it?" he said.

Exasperated, Crina tidied the papers Razvan had thrown down and placed them in a neat stack on the desk. She locked her eyes directly on his.

"Mister Petrescu"—she always addressed her boss formally when she wanted to make an important point— "of course I love and respect you and please understand I do indeed treasure our language, but we must be ready and willing to speak many languages if we are to attend to the needs of our guests. We are all fortunate they come from everywhere to stay at your beautiful hotel and experience Romania's gorgeous scenery."

Razvan bristled at her words. While deep down he acknowledged Crina was correct—he understood she always was—these were still unpleasant facts he preferred to ignore. He pulled the cigarette from his mouth, allowing him to speak freely.

"If they want to use English, they should stay at an English hotel."

Satisfied he has made his point, Razvan patted Crina's hand and walked across the hotel's grand lobby. The spacious front room was no less majestic than the building's exterior. Granite and hardwoods lined every square centimeter of the floor. Massive columns wrapped in a flourish of carved swans and ferns launched from the polished floor to the sculpted ceiling. Oversized portraits of Russian President Leonid Brezhnev and the recently elected Romanian leader Ceausescu sat high above the sturdy oak reception desk. Each image had eyes which followed a person no matter where one stood. The roving eyes were a perfect metaphor for the lives of common Romanian citizens living under constant surveillance by the police and perhaps their own neighbors. At the far end of the room, sitting to the side of the reception desk, an elegant set of hardwood stairs lined with oil paintings of mountain landscapes swept upward. Romanian folk music gently filled the air. Razvan paused at the foot of the staircase and finally lit his dangling Gauloise before turning back to face Crina.

"I understand your point, Crina. You are a smart girl. I am a—" He struggled to find the right word to express his feelings. "What is the phrase? Ah! I am a lucky man to have you here."

Having said his final words on the matter, Razvan pulled in a lungful of nicotine and winked at

Crina before climbing the stairs. Crina's head tilted and a smile appeared accompanied by raised eyebrows. Compliments were not something her boss was fond of handing out.

Wheezing as he reached the top steps, Razvan stopped to catch his breath. Too many years of sucking down cheap Romanian tobacco had blackened his lungs. He mistakenly believed switching to French sticks would produce a smoother smoke and actually clear his lungs in the process. Razvan had been raised in a tiny house that lacked both an indoor toilet and running water. His parents had been illiterate and his own formal education had ended when he reached the age of fifteen. The village had provided an endless monologue of home remedies and medicinal advice delivered by grandmothers and priests. Razvan leaned on their opinions when he decided smoking a French Gauloise would improve his deteriorating health.

The portly man walked down the narrow hallway leading away from the stairs. Guest rooms lined the hall on either side and the old wooden floors creaked under the green-and-blue swirled design of the polyester carpet as he ambled forward with his sizable mass. While the lobby had exuded elegance from floor to ceiling, the hallway was Cold War chic. Ostensibly, Razvan had run out of funds when renovation had reached the second floor, but it was impossible to confirm if this rumor was true. In his mind, he believed a hotel should be about first appearances and opulence in public places. Private areas were not for crowds and, therefore, spending money on them was wasteful. People went to their rooms to close their eyes and sleep, but when they were in the lobby, the restaurant, or the indoor pool, closing their eyes was the furthest thing from their mind. The memories of the public spaces were the experiences people would take home with them.

A short distance down the hall, the hotel's maintenance man was using a manual drill handle and spade bit to noisily make a hole in the door of one of the rooms. Brightly polished brass numbers identified the room as number 215.

Toma Galu appeared like the vision of every woman's dream. He was tall and handsome with a commanding mustache and speckled gray hair which made him seem older than his thirty-seven years. His clothes were the uniform of a handyman, but he wore the overalls and canvas shirt far better than most. Under his loose-fitting blue shirt was a wall of muscle and a selection of tattoos he had decorated himself with while serving in the Romanian army. Technically, getting inked was a violation of military code, but as long as a man proved himself to be a worthwhile soldier, the commanders turned a blind eye. Toma had indeed been an upstanding man in service to his country and, at the tender age of seventeen, had fought in several battles toward the end of the war.

"Toma!" Razvan said. "I hope our guest is not in their room while you make all this noise and dust!"

"Of course not, sir. All the guests on this floor are at dinner."

"Good."

Having finished drilling, Toma dropped the drill handle into a cloth tool bag at his feet and retrieved a small brass cylinder from the same bag. Razvan moved forward and peeked through the small hole Toma had drilled. Toma politely tapped on Razvan's shoulder and the old man stepped aside, allowing him to slide the brass cylinder into the hole. Using his fist, Toma rapped the cylinder into place before pushing the tube flush with his thumb.

"When will you be done putting in these peepers? Is this what they are called? Soon, I hope."

Toma pointed to the room to the left. "I have only one more to do after this one."

Razvan blew a cloud of aromatic smoke into the air before turning to leave. "Well, make it quick. I need the work finished and this hall clean before the guests return to their rooms. Understood?"

Toma was numb to these demands. This was not the first time the old hotel owner had ordered him around, but he was smart enough not to speak out. "Of course, Razvan. It will be done. They will never know I was here."

As he walked down the hall, Razvan stopped at a knee-high metal cylinder, the top of which was an ashtray. He took a final long drag on his cigarette before crushing the remainder into the ashtray. He glanced back to check on Toma and let the smoke drift out of his mouth and nose. Despite the warning he had from his doctor to stop smoking, he lived for moments like these—standing in the hallway of his hotel breathing fire while he monitored people working for him. The scenario made him feel Herculean.

"Make it so," he said before continuing to the stairs.

Toma's cheeks became taught, and he closed his eyes as he tried to control his anger toward the hotelier and his own job. While he enjoyed finally having decent employment after a few years in prison for theft—a crime he was innocent of—he was still troubled by being treated like a low-class worker. In addition to being a decorated soldier, Toma had graduated from a prestigious Romanian university with a degree in chemistry, but the university's curriculum had done little to prepare him for the difficulties of finding employment in a deteriorating communist economy. For Toma, the polish had worn off the manifesto Marx had promised was the way forward. Not only was a family unable to buy bread, but jobs were also nonexistent. When he learned the castle was being renovated, he hiked for two days from his city through the forest to reach the busy construction site. Within a day or two, he had proven to be a knowledgeable and strong worker and as the hotel neared completion, he asked Razvan to keep him on. The old man had agreed and Toma became the Teleki's first official employee.

Razvan stepped from the stairs and walked proudly across the polished floor of the lobby to the hotel's restaurant. He stood for a moment in the doorway, viewing the guests attending to their dinner.

Simon King

Like the lobby, the restaurant featured marble columns and oak walls. Numerous tables filled the room in a pattern that was both intimate and logical. Each table had a starched white tablecloth and silverware that shined bright thanks to the room's ample lighting. An efficient bar occupied one wall of the space, behind which was an impressive collection of wines and liquors from the best vineyards and regions of Europe.

Satisfied that paying guests occupied many of the tables, Razvan crossed the restaurant to the kitchen, a relatively tiny space located behind a pair of swinging metal doors. Each door had a small window to check if anyone was about to enter or exit the kitchen. Of course, these openings were not necessary to the small number of staff who worked the restaurant since they were all experienced enough to enter the food preparation area through the right-hand door and exit through the restaurant using the other. Sadly, while the room may have been his kitchen in his hotel, Razvan routinely ignored the unwritten rules and used whichever door suited him.

The hotel's kitchen was modest but immaculately clean. The food prep area was always a source of wonderful aromas that wafted throughout the restaurant and flowed into the lobby. The warm perfume of fresh bread greeted the guests in the morning, and in the afternoon the aroma of *mici*—cabbage rolls and grilled minced meat creations—wafted through the room. The evening meals provided the most spirituous perfumes with local fish poached in grape leaves or perhaps the

22

ever-popular *drob de miel,* which westerners ordered as lamb-drop, filling the air and beckoning guests from their rooms to the restaurant.

The undersized facility forced anyone who worked in the kitchen to be efficient with their movements and actions. It was obvious to hotel guests Razvan had designed the public spaces to appeal to one's eye, but during construction, he had always been troubled by how much expense it took to renovate this tiny space. Stainless steel was not inexpensive and this room glistened with the polished metal. The refrigerators, gas stoves, and oversized sinks were especially expensive. Regardless of the size of the room, Razvan had been proud of the finished product. An oversized food preparation table formed the centerpiece of the kitchen. On this particular day, several knives and other utensils lay at rest on the wooden table. Brass pots and cast-iron pans of various shapes and sizes lined the walls of the room. Still more hung from a stainless rack hanging above the table. A multi-burner gas stove—purchased from a now-closed Parisian restaurant—blazed furiously with several saucepans of food bubbling to culinary perfection.

The chef, Ilam Izri, was in his early thirties, having arrived in Romania only two years previously from Morocco. He had come highly recommended and brought with him dishes unfamiliar to the more traditional Romanian menu. Shorter than Toma, Ilam had a tightly-cropped beard and walked with a slight limp, the result of a nasty fight in his teenage years. One only had to catch him in the kitchen for a brief moment to understand he had total command over the space he worked in. He was the king and this was his kingdom. Like any king, he had a crown and Ilam wore his *toque blanche* with pride. The headwear, however, did little to hide his frequent, volatile outbursts.

Satisfied Ilam had everything under control and unwilling to spark a fight with the chef as would often happen given the slightest misplaced word, Razvan turned to leave through the kitchen's swinging door. At the same moment, the door swung toward him, almost knocking him backward.

"Otilia! Be careful!" Razvan said.

He had no reason to be angry with the waitress as she was using the proper door, and he was not. The protocol of which door to use was well known to anyone who had worked in a busy industrial kitchen. Perhaps more than any other space in the hotel, the kitchen had strict rules—some dictated by Romanian law and others borne from decades of common knowledge.

"Oh my, Razvan," said Otilia. "So sorry, I did not expect someone to be passing through the wrong door." She was sure her sarcasm would be lost on the fat old man.

Otilia Sava, the hotel's only waitress in the winter months, always did her best to hide her anger at people thinking or acting in a manner not to her liking; and the list of those she did not like was lengthy. In Otilia's mind, everyone but herself lacked common sense. Razvan had proved her point by his inability to properly use well-marked directions on something as simple as a door.

"No, you have the only reason to be in here," Razvan said. "I must not be in the way of the two of you feeding our guests." He moved again to the wrong door but stood for a moment considering his actions before he shifted his mass to the right. Proud he was making the correct choice, he pushed the door open and marched out in almost presidential fashion.

Otilia and Ilam exchanged a glance. Neither believed their boss was apologizing.

Like Ilam, Otilia had arrived in Romania only recently from her parents' home in Ukraine. She had been a satisfactory, if uninterested, student and everyone thought she would attend university in Kyiv, but she wanted her freedom. The time had come to leave her strict parents behind and explore the vast world she had read so much about in black-market European magazines. She was ready to live in a world without her abusive and demanding boyfriend, who she had abandoned without a single word of explanation.

Barely twenty, Otilia was as thin as a twig with flowing hair tied neatly into a tight bun. While Ilam was proud of his chef's uniform, Otilia resented the clothes of a waitress. They made her feel like a servant and someone who deserved to be ignored. She anxiously awaited each evening when she returned to her room in the basement of the hotel and exchanged the unflattering white cotton calf-length dress and flat-soled shoes for one of the miniskirts her mother had always complained were too short and more fitting of a prostitute. Her parents would have frowned at her new style of wearing sheer blouses with a dark bra. "Have you no modesty?" her mother would scream. In these clothes, with her hair down and a pair of bright heels on her feet, Otilia felt sexy and able to ignore those who stared down their nose at her.

"These are for table four, right?"

"Yep. Don't let them complain. My food is perfect," Ilam said.

Otilia picked up the plates of prepared meals from the warming station and headed for the proper swinging door. This time, as her hands were full, and she refused to run into Razvan if he had insisted on returning, she took an extra second to peer through the door's window to make sure no one was standing in her way out to the restaurant. She thought trivialities like labeling doors and providing windows in them were all so unnecessary if people would just follow the simple rules of life.

She walked across the restaurant with the plates of hot food balanced with a skill developed from experience. Weaving past empty tables, she headed toward a small table occupied by two men enjoying glasses of red wine. She always put on a smile for her customers, which was an effective disguise for the contempt she held inside. To her, they were all wealthy snobs who could afford to stay at luxury resorts and order more food than they had any intention of eating. Occasionally, a guest would surprise her with a different view on life. She had already determined the men at this table were such an exception. Of course, the older gentleman and his companion was wealthy. This was evident and not a concern. The problem was they were homosexuals, something still buried deep in Romania's closet. Favoring the comfort of one's own sex was an unknown lifestyle for Otilia, but one which excited the young woman. In her brief experience with lovemaking, she had enjoyed the company of only a few men—all boys in her opinion—but in her mind, she had not yet ruled out experimenting.

"Gentlemen, your dinner."

"Ah! Delightful!" Everett said. "I am certain this fine meal will shame anything from good old England where the food is insipid to the taste and destructive to the constitution."

Everett Cook hid a sturdy frame under his almost seventy-year-old skin. As had been his passion for more than four decades, Everett wore Savile Row's finest head-to-toe, and he was never seen in public without a shocking pink pocket square. More than a fashion statement, the bold piece of silk was an obvious declaration of his lifestyle in a world not ready to accept him for what he was. He also considered himself naked if he did not have his custom-made walking stick, which was apparently more for show than to aid in his forward progress. The cane came from a stout British walnut tree and an elaborate bronze animal's head topped it off giving him something distinctive and sturdy to wrap his hand around.

The elderly Brit had a storied, if somewhat unknown, past serving his king and country during the war and remaining in Her Majesty's service ever since. Rumor bounced around he had involved a young male researcher in some questionable personal behavior occurring in a back room at Bletchley Park in 1948, but once again, and as was always the case in events involving Everett Cook, no one was aware of what the truth might actually be. His stellar record with the government allowed all sorts of inconsistencies to be swept beneath the thick Indian rug of national security. Everett had been raised a strict Protestant by his school teacher mum and Bible-pounding father who was not above using the Good Book as a weapon when putting Everett in his place. He often wondered if his sexual orientation could be explained by his abusive upbringing.

Otilia waited while Everett moved his ornate and slender walking stick to the other side of his chair thus giving her better access to the table. She slid a plate of roast beef and steamed vegetables in front of Everett before moving to the other side of the table where she set down a plate of food for the younger man. Inquisitive was Everett's nature, and he leaned in to look across the table.

"What have you ordered, dear boy?"

"The usual, Ev. Salmon and rice."

This overly casual abbreviation never sat well with Everett.

"Please Christian, you promised, Everett, not Ev. Never."

His consort responded in the only way a man of his training could—flashing a thousand-dollar smile.

"My apologies. Everett."

Everett extended a thin, pale hand across the table and wrapped his fingers around Christian's sturdy hand. The contrast between old and young and wiry and muscular was dramatic.

"Oh Christian, my dear. I could never be cross with you."

Christian Caine was in his late twenties and Hollywood handsome. He attracted plenty of women with his looks and laughter but men also went a bit weak in his presence. He came from a wealthy family who owned a beautiful home in London's Notting Hill and a weekend getaway, as his father referred to the expansive estate, in the Scottish Highlands. This second home was nothing short of a castle on more than a thousand acres. Christian had enjoyed his younger years learning to hunt fox and deer on the property. At the age of eighteen, an impassioned argument had erupted over a hopeful union between Christian and a beautiful French woman. Not only was he not interested in an arranged marriage, he took the opportunity to announce he was gay. The next day, Christian's name disappeared from his father's will and he became *persona non grata* in the family forever.

Christian dressed not for himself, but for his older lover. Everett had first seen the young man at London Fashion Week the past September, and he wasted no time in inviting the up-and-coming model on a variety of brief outings. These had started with an evening of theater and dinner but soon evolved to overnights at Everett's cozy cottage in the Lake District. The holidays were always paid for by Everett who had a bottomless wallet, which was fortunate for the younger man as Christian had almost nothing to his name. Without Everett to keep him fed and well clothed, he would be pulling on the dole when not walking the runway for a few pounds.

Seeing the two men had all they needed, Otilia left their table and moved to one in the far corner of the room where a statuesque young woman sat alone. She was another guest who interested Otilia as the waitress had only seen a handful of black women in her life. In school, Otilia had learned of the mistreatment of blacks in America, a situation leading the Soviet Union to actively recruit black Americans to Russia, a country that proclaimed racism did not exist under Stalin and Communism. Regardless of the politics involved, this woman fascinated Otilia, and she wondered what had compelled her to travel alone to the Teleki in the middle of winter.

Anne-Marie Paris was every man's dream and the cause of more than a few women's jealousies. A tad shy of one meter eighty and clocking in at no more than fifty-two kilos, Anne-Marie had been a high-profile fashion model for years. She had walked the catwalks of Paris, Milan, New York, and London wearing haute couture from the world's most famous designers and had appeared on Vogue covers in almost every country that had a localized version of the publication. Her flawless ebony skin and perfect measurements made her a favorite of swimwear and lingerie ateliers who paid her top dollar to showcase their creations. But one day, she gave up the life of a model and went to medical school. The decision was quite sudden and no explanation was forthcoming, but rumors about a prominent fashion photographer becoming a bit too touchy-feely leading to a heavy tripod being rammed into his crotch hard enough that he required a week in the hospital rang more than a bit true.

"How is everything, miss?" said Otilia. "Anything you need?"

Anne-Marie accepted the pleasantries for what they were and smiled gracefully. "Everything is fine. Thank you. Well, perhaps another carafe of water when you have a chance."

Anne-Marie was not antisocial; she was capable of being friends with anyone and partied to an extent that left others face down in their vodka. But tonight, she was lost in thought about a tricky task which lay ahead. She told herself this was her only dilemma, but she had longing in her heart. More than anything else, Anne-Marie desperately wanted to be married and produce an endless stream of children. She had been raised by a single mother who took care of Anne-Marie and her five older brothers in a tiny squat of a home with no more than a few coins to her name. Her mother had washed the clothes of wealthy white folks who lived in a part of the city she herself was forbidden to visit. When Anne-Marie had been discovered by a modeling scout, her meteoric rise to the status of a world-famous model had rescued the family from extreme poverty and provided her mother the life she deserved. Despite the hardships of her childhood, Anne-Marie had many positive remembrances of playing with her brothers and wanted to have her own children so as to relive those memories.

Otilia acknowledged Anne-Marie's request and turned away, letting the smile drop from her face as fast as the expression had appeared. She walked to another table where a well-dressed couple sat. Anyone listening was aware their conversation was stressed.

"Remind me again, Dan, what do I pay you for?" Isabella Manson said.

This question was not new to Dan Steel. But before he answered, Isabella continued her complaint.

"You're supposed to be a brilliant agent, right? My agent, in fact. So, when was the last time you got me cast in anything other than some third-rate shit?"

"Pay me? Isabella... I only make money when you do. That's how this works. I want you to work so I can make money."

Isabella Manson was a still-beautiful American actress, pushing life well beyond her best days on the screen. She understood the value of keeping up appearances in case a fan or, better yet, an in-demand director or hungry producer might catch sight of her. She was dressed to kill, from her stark white André Courrèges go-go boots and Givenchy dress to her expertly coiffed hairstyle. Isabella had signed a long-term contract with RKO Pictures in Hollywood in early 1954. The agreement ended abruptly a few years later when RKO went bankrupt. By then she was a household name and the offers came fast and furious for several years until just as dramatically, she was no longer an *it* girl. Theatergoers were a fickle bunch and Isabella found herself considering films no studio or agent ever would have insulted her with only a year before. But she was a fighter, and fight she did, keeping her name in the press, even if Isabella Manson was no longer on the front page of the Hollywood Reporter or Variety.

Her half-attentive agent, Dan Steel, could have been an actor himself with his chiseled looks and blinding teeth, but he recognized early on plenty of money could be made representing film actors and actresses. He dressed the part of a successful talent agent with a spotless tailored suit and open neck silk shirt. His slick-backed hair was almost as shiny as his highly-polished five-hundred-dollar shoes. Like many in the industry, Dan was a known womanizer who took advantage of his position to bed an endless train of young girls hoping to become the next Marilyn Monroe. Flattering promises were made in the bedroom but Dan forgot them almost as the words left his mouth and the women would soon be, at best, mixing milkshakes at a lowly drive-thru, or if things had really gone south, traveling on a bus back to Mom and Dad to some miserable town in the Midwest.

Dan took advantage of Isabella's momentary silence to mop up the final bits of rice from his evening meal. Finished, he dabbed his mouth with a napkin and dropped the soiled cloth on his plate before looking across the table at Isabella.

"Isabella, please... you know the problem."

This was the segue Isabella needed to continue her assault.

"Don't tell me. Wait, what were your words? Ah yes, age brings wisdom and skill. What do those young bitches have I don't? Huh? Nothing! That's what! Let them lay down on the damn studio couch and show their stuff. Isabella Manson is an actress, not a whore! Remember that!"

Otilia arrived at their table and made her presence known in time to lower the tension.

"How are you doing with your food?" she said. "May I bring you anything else? Some dessert perhaps? Our chef makes a delicious *savarină* cake. I promise this treat will give you wonderful dreams tonight."

Otilia began gathering the empty plates. Her pulse pounded in her slender neck as she listened to the spoiled Americans sitting in front of her. Where she had accepted Everett for his out-of-the-norm lifestyle and Anne-Marie had made her feel comfortable with her beauty, these two were the type of guests who made her want to pack her few belongings and return to Ukraine.

Dan rubbed his temples to ease the throbbing brought on by his client's constant nagging. Headaches were an ailment Isabella often induced. Dessert was not what he needed. No cake, or pie, or other heavy pastry would numb the inevitable.

"A double vodka, please."

"Of course, sir, and for you, ma'am?"

"I would like—"

34

"She's fine," Dan said. "No more, thank you."

"As you wish, sir," Otilia said.

Dan's declarations never sat well with Isabella. He had often stepped in and made demands like this before. Perhaps Dan thought Isabella would recognize he had her best wishes at heart, but his inability to provide powerful scripts and opportunities was becoming increasingly irritating as the months of no decent acting offers wore on. The reality was all too much, she hadn't been busting her ass as a successful actress for two decades to have some slime-ball agent dictate what she should or should not drink, or eat, or do with her free time. As Otilia stepped away, Isabella did nothing to hide her anger.

"Fine? Do you call this fine? I don't think so!" Her narrowed eyes and sneering mouth cut into Dan. The time had come to show him who the boss was. "Excuse me, miss, please bring me some of that cake. What was the name again?"

Otilia returned to the table. Somehow, she predicted the American would change her mind. From experience, she understood this to always be the case.

"*Savarină* is quite traditional in Romania. You will not be disappointed."

"Well, at least the dessert will not disappoint me," said Isabella as she eyed Dan with contempt.

"You're gonna get fat. No one wants a pudgy actress."

"I'm thin and no one wants me so who knows, perhaps a fat Isabella Manson is what America wants on the silver screen. Perhaps that's why they call it the big screen." She was proud of those words and a quirky smile filled her face.

Their argument faded into the background as Otilia walked toward the kitchen only to be stopped short by the sight of two women waiting at the entrance to the restaurant. Convinced the Americans could wait for their vodka and dessert, Otilia went to greet the new diners.

The women were a mother and daughter, or more accurately, a stepmother and stepdaughter. Hungarian by birth, Márta Karády was in her forties. A controlling woman who had no time for fools and foolish pastimes, Márta prided herself on dressing modestly and acting with utmost decorum at all times. She was the type of woman who frightened men as they remembered everything bad about their own mothers in her persona. Before marrying the father of her stepdaughter, Márta had worked as an official in the Hungarian communist party. While in this position, she earned a reputation as a taskmaster who demanded excellence from her subordinates and was known to complain despite a job being completed as required and on time.

The young girl could not have been more different than Márta. Lilla Karády was in the last of her teenage years and she relished the freedom this provided her. She was born in Ukraine where she lived most of her life before her mother died in a tragic hit-and-run. Suspicions were raised the homicide may actually have been a planned killing by an angry mafia-type in retribution for a major real estate deal involving her father that had gone sour, but nothing was ever proved. After the death, her father had insisted on leaving Ukraine and relaunched his real estate business with immense success in Hungary, where he soon met and married Márta. Too soon and too quickly, in Lilla's opinion. As a form of rebellion, Lilla began dressing like the teenagers in French fashion advertisements and contraband American rock-and-roll magazines. In addition, she did nothing to hold back her carnal desires for men; men much older than herself. While her father brushed her odd predilections off as a fad and only warned her not to get pregnant, Márta accepted rehabilitating Lilla and making a lady out of her a personal responsibility. This was the source of endless agitation between the two.

"Good evening ladies, may I seat you for dinner?"

"Yes, my dear," said Márta. "That would be wonderful."

This brief initial meeting was all that was necessary for Otilia to develop a distaste for the two. This was especially true with respect to Lilla who reminded Otilia of everything she was missing by being a waitress. Regardless of the inner voice telling her to frown at the women, she smiled and escorted Márta and Lilla to a table near where Dan Steel and Isabella Manson now sat in silence.

As they approached the table, Márta glanced at Dan Steel and her mood abruptly changed.

"I'm so sorry, do you have another table? Perhaps something closer to the window?" Her stance was intimidating, and she was not about to take no for an answer.

"Of course, ma'am."

These demands were the reason Otilia held so much contempt toward the guests. Nothing was ever up to the mark. For a brief moment, she actually sympathized with Lilla for having to be with this woman. What must it be like? she thought.

Otilia led the ladies to Márta's desired location. On the way, they passed Alejandro Serrat. The Spaniard was dining alone and had pushed his unfinished meal to the side as he diligently wrote in a weathered notebook. Márta considered him for a moment and decided he wore the clothes of a revolutionary. She was not far from the truth. Alejandro had been born in 1936 while his father was off fighting in the Spanish Civil War. Like more than 350,000 other Spanish men, his father did not return. A few years later, when President Franco announced his support of Hitler, Alejandro's mother started publishing an anti-government newsletter. This speedily landed her in prison and Alejandro was shipped to Catalonia to live with an aunt. His mother did not survive her sentence and as a result, Alejandro grew to hate everything the fascist government stood for. Like his mother, he became a writer and his pro-democracy essays were published internationally under a nom de plume and in secrecy. Franco wanted the mysterious author found and punished, but so far, Alejandro had managed to avoid the fate of his mother and father.

On Alejandro's table sat a small leather satchel from which a collection of papers and pencils tumbled forth. As Lilla walked slowly past, Alejandro breathed in her perfume and his gaze jumped from his writing to the young woman. This was not the first time he had been entranced by the fragrance and the aroma brought back pleasant, rather decadent, memories. As he checked out Lilla walking to her table and taking a seat, he was quite pleased by her movements and a sly but welcoming smile appeared on his face.

The ladies sat at a comfortable table below an enormous window overlooking the snow-covered parking lot. On a nicer day, guests witnessed the expanse of rocky and precipitous mountaintops set before them. But not today.

"Much better, thank you," said Márta.

Lilla had chosen her seat with care as she had a direct view past Márta toward Alejandro. Lilla did her best to make sure he realized she was nearby and available. She need not have tried so hard because he was well aware of her presence.

"Perhaps you would like to start with a glass of wine?"

"Oh, yes, please. I shall have a glass of rosé and the young lady will have a glass of tomato juice."

Márta reached into her purse and pulled out a bright red crochet needle attached to a partially-finished project.

"Oh, your work is beautiful! You are so creative. I have always wanted to learn to crochet." For once, Otilia's interest in a guest was real. Her mother had knitted her many wonderful winter sweaters when she was a young child and now, she wanted to learn to knit, or crotchet, or sew her own clothes. She loved the styles western women wore, but they were either unavailable in Romania or the black-market prices were outrageous. Otilia was sure she could compete with the most beautiful women in Paris and New York if only she had the proper clothing.

"Crocheting is relaxing," said Márta, "but sometimes not. Starting a project is fun and full of hope and finishing one is simply wonderful. But it is the days, or weeks, in between that can be frustrating."

"I can only imagine." Otilia handed Márta and Lilla menus and left for the kitchen.

"Márta, why must you? I am not a child. I do drink, you know?" This was not the first time Lilla had clashed with Márta over drinking alcohol or almost everything for that matter.

Despite Lilla not being her own child, she wasted no time in attempting to take control when the girl's father would not. This always led to heated disagreements.

"I do not know that. And, you will always be a child. My child." Márta examined her crocheting and adjusted the needle to the correct position.

"You are not my mother!" Lilla's voice raised uncomfortably. She was sure Alejandro was hearing the conversation.

"Perhaps not," Márta said as she expertly moved the needle through the yarn. "But for now, for this trip, you will do me the pleasure of pretending it to be the case. Furthermore, my darling, as far as others are concerned, I am your mother, and I deserve to be referred to in that manner. Remember, first names are for friends and associates. And you, are neither."

"Of course, mother." Her words carried more than a hint of distaste for the woman. This time, she wanted her attractive Spanish neighbor to understand she could be assertive. She imagined Alejandro might prefer a woman who took charge. This was the first time Lilla had traveled with only Márta and not her father. She was already regretting the decision. *Any benefit I hoped for by coming to this hotel had better outweigh the pain of having to live under the watchful eye of this woman*, she thought.

"Listen, Márta, you must be honest with yourself, and understand I do have—" She paused to find the right word. This was a technique Lilla's father had taught her to avoid putting her foot in her mouth. "I have certain activities. Things I like to do that do not and, I promise you, will never involve you." She was addressing her stepmother but her eyes were on Alejandro.

Márta was aware Lilla's focus was wandering. This was a problem she had witnessed in the young girl ever since she was introduced to her. She did not expect the girl to be a prude or ignore boys, but she wished Lilla would stay within a healthy age range when flirting. As a younger woman, Márta had made numerous mistakes in her own romantic relationships, and she wanted to pass her knowledge along to her stepdaughter. The young woman, however, had turned the experience into an endless battle.

"Perhaps, but for now they must be"—Márta paused as she too thought how best to finish her sentence without sounding overbearing— "Contained. Are we clear?"

At that moment, Otilia returned with a small glass of tomato juice and the glass of rosé.

"Have you ladies had a chance to consider the menu?"

"Oh, not yet. Lilla, darling, what will you be having?"

Márta placed her crotchet work on the table with care. She took pride in her various knitting and crochet projects and secretly hoped one day Lilla might ask her to teach her.

As Márta considered the menu, the room was abruptly flooded with a bright light coming from outside. For all intents and purposes, one would think a searchlight had been focused on the room. Márta turned to consider what was happening on the other side of the snow-covered window. She shielded her eyes as the glare grew in intensity. The headlights of a rapidly approaching car flashed through the blowing snow. The car appeared to be advancing unnecessarily fast on the hotel and seemed as though it might crash through the window and into the restaurant. At the last moment, the car came to a sliding halt in front of the window.

"Oh my!" said Otilia. "I didn't think anyone else would make it here in this storm." Of course, what she meant was she had hoped no other guests needed her attention. Another hotel guest asking for special treatment and keeping her from enjoying her own life was not what Otilia wanted.

"Impressive, I would say," said Alejandro. "Or perhaps a madman."

The restaurant became silent as all the guests focused on the solitary car outside. Although the Mercedes was now parked and stationary, its lights lingered far too long appearing to interrogate the diners inside—asking each of them what they were eating and who they were with. The lights finally blinked off, making the scene outside once again black. The only sound was snow softly hitting the window. Moments later, the restaurant returned to normal with quiet conversations and the clinking of knives and forks against fine bone china. Perhaps the guests believed whoever had arrived was of no significance.

Simon King

Chapter 3

Polina Tolkunova sat for a moment, gathering her thoughts. The past hour had been an ultimate test of her driving abilities, but now she would need to lean upon a rather different set of skills. She reached into her purse and retrieved a tube of lipstick. The bag would always have a selection of two or three colors to match a variety of outfits, but for this trip, she decided to bring only a single color. Polina spun the tube open revealing a dazzling pillar of red gloss. Red was a color she was partial to whether it be lipstick, underwear—which always matched—a purse, or a pair of impossible heels. Looking into the car's rearview mirror, she applied the lipstick methodically, smacked her lips together, and satisfied with the result, returned the tube to her purse.

The vehicle's headlights gave Polina an unadulterated view of the restaurant. She was the only one in the audience and all the diners were on a stage. She counted the guests and considered the number to be appropriate for the season and weather conditions. Polina reviewed the diners as they winced and shaded their eyes, hoping for a clearer view of who had arrived under such horrid circumstances. Having decided the patrons had had enough, Polina switched off the engine and the headlights quickly faded. *Now I am on stage*, Polina thought.

After removing the keys from the ignition, Polina opened the car door and stepped out, into the swirling snow. Her elegant red leather fur-trimmed boots sunk deep into the white carpet. She had bought them while on a recent assignment in Italy, and she loved how they went above her knees. Standing up, she pulled her full-length white mink coat close to her chest. After grabbing her purse and a small suitcase from the car, she made her way through the snowdrifts toward the hotel's entrance. Polina was runway-ready even when trudging through knee-deep snow.

The lobby offered a blast of warm air as Polina opened the oversized doors. She was not alone near the door for the blizzard accompanied her with a wave of frenzied flakes. She pushed the door closed behind her and the snow lingered in the air for a moment before dropping to the floor of the lobby and quickly melting into small, almost circular puddles. Polina stomped her feet to remove any offending snow. She did this both out of respect for the hotel and to guarantee anyone in the room would appreciate her Italian purchase. As if her elegant coat and boots and the manner in which she walked weren't enough to convince them, the cherry-red lipstick and her obvious beauty ensured any man or woman would admit she was a knockout. The fact her lip color and her purse matched her footwear sealed the package.

Crina had been diligently watching her new guest arrive since the glimmer of headlights first appeared coming up the hotel's long driveway. Only one more person was listed for a stay that night, so she understood this must be the woman from Russia who had called earlier in the morning to make a last-minute reservation. At the time, Crina thought asking for a room in such a manner at a mountain resort in the middle of a Romanian winter was strange. A quick check of the weather report would have indicated driving to the mountains was a foolish enterprise not to be taken lightly. *Some people lack common sense*, Crina thought to herself.

As was her way of greeting every guest, Crina smiled wide as Polina glided across the polished floor toward her. Secretly, she admired everything about this woman, and who wouldn't?

"Miss Tolkunova, I presume," Crina said. "I am so surprised and happy you were able to make it! We wouldn't have been upset if you had needed to cancel your reservation. It would be completely understandable."

Well, Crina and the staff wouldn't have minded, but Razvan would have been another matter. He never liked cancellations and considered them an insult.

Polina appreciated the smile and pleasant voice that greeted her. This was not always the case at the hotels she so often had to stay at while on assignment. As she glanced around, she was taken by the fact this hotel was far superior to any she had been required to utilize before. Typically, the accommodations selected for her were on the low end of acceptable. She had come to expect and accept thin walls, squeaky mattresses, no hot water, and food that was questionable at best. She wasn't sure, however, if having a hotel of the caliber she now stood in meant the job would be any easier.

"It was a challenge, but yes I made it and yes, I am Polina Tolkunova."

Crina examined the paperwork on her desk, pretending to search for Polina's reservation. Of course, she didn't need to waste any time doing this, but she wanted her to believe the Teleki may have other guests still on their way. She had learned one must never appear desperate in the hotel business. An air of confidence and professionalism was required at all times. This hadn't always been easy, as some guests had the inborn ability to make her life a living hell.

"Now, Miss Tolkunova, we have you here for one night. Is that correct?"

"Yes, I believe so."

"Excellent! You may, of course, pay when you are finished with your stay, but as you may know, I will need to keep your passport until you leave. It is our Romanian law."

"Of course. I understand. I prefer to pay in advance if that's acceptable."

"Yes, that's fine. Let me prepare a bill for you. One moment."

Polina never paid at the end of a hotel stay. Her work often meant she would leave a hotel in the middle of the night or with close to no warning. Rather than risk having to wait when time was of the essence, she had taken to paying upfront to avoid any difficulty or delay.

Polina reached again into her purse, being careful not to reveal some of the bag's more questionable contents. Her passport fell into her hand as she pushed deeper into her purse. Pulling the document out, she handed it to Crina.

"This isn't my first visit to Romania, but this is the first time I have traveled into the mountains. Quite beautiful, at least what wasn't obscured by the blizzard."

"I'm relieved the road was clear enough for you to come here. The driving must have been challenging."

"Yes, I suppose it was. But then again, what isn't challenging in our lives nowadays?" She gave Crina a reassuring smile meant to relax the hotel's manager.

Having recorded the needed information in the Teleki's register, Crina reached behind her to the rows of room keys and selected one, which she handed to Polina. The key was a brightly polished skeleton key attached to an oval of shiny brass with the room number etched into the disk. As with everything at the resort, Razvan had complained at the cost to produce the keys and their fobs but deep down, he was proud of them. In fact, he was proud of every tiny detail at Hotel Teleki.

"I have you on the second floor, room 215. We are still serving dinner in the dining room if you would like something. Your meal is included in the cost of the room. Here's your bill."

Crina presented Polina with a bill for the room. Accommodation and breakfast came to forty leu. Polina pulled out a small leather wallet that matched the purse perfectly. She had, of course, purchased them as a set. Polina handed over fifty leu.

"Please distribute the balance to your staff."

"Thank you, Miss Tolkunova. That is quite generous."

Polina accepted the key and absentmindedly rubbed the brass fob between her fingers. She appreciated the solid metal and promptly realized she hadn't eaten for hours. The stress of driving in the storm had occupied her mind, but now she was famished.

"May I have food delivered to my room?"

Crina checked her wristwatch, but before she could answer, Polina's attention was elsewhere. At this moment, Dan and Isabella, having finished their meal, stepped from the restaurant and into the lobby. A smile crossed Dan's face as he eyed Polina at the front desk. It was unclear if this was a twinkle of recognition or—as Isabella presumed—one of lust.

"Seriously?" Isabella said. "Any woman you won't hit on?" She wanted to be even more vocal on the matter, but she bit her tongue and decided to reprimand him later.

Polina eyed the Americans cautiously as they continued past her to the nearby stairs. Was this him? The man she came here for? He met the physical description, but something wasn't quite right. No matter. Now wasn't the proper time to concern herself with such details.

Isabella started up the stairs first, giving Dan an opportunity to glance back one more time at Polina. She did her best to ignore him. If he was who she thought him to be, Polina was sure an occasion would present itself. Polina realized she hadn't paid attention to Crina's answer to her dining question.

"I'm so sorry, did you say in-room dining was an option tonight?"

"Yes, you'll find a menu in your room. The chef will be preparing food for another hour. Otilia, our waitress, will bring your meal to your room. You can call from your room to the restaurant to place your order. You'll find instructions inside the menu."

"Thank you, that will be perfect." Polina turned and walked toward the stairs but stopped abruptly and returned to the front desk.

"Yes, Miss Tolkunova?"

"I'm sorry. I remembered something. I need to make an international call. Can this be arranged?"

"Normally, yes, of course. But this storm must have done damage to the telephone service. I am hopeful the phone will be working as soon as the blizzard ends."

"And when will that be?"

Crina continued to smile, but inside she wondered why guests often asked questions that were impossible to answer. "The weather report says the worst of will be over by tomorrow morning. But in these mountains, the information isn't always useful, or for that matter, truthful."

"I'm confused. You said to use the phone to order my food, but I can't use the phone for calls outside the hotel?"

"Oh yes, I'm afraid our phone system is a bit antiquated. The phone for inside the hotel operates on a different circuit than what you would use to call elsewhere. I don't quite understand the whole setup myself, but I assure you I'll let you know as soon as outside service becomes available."

Polina tapped her room key on the counter in frustration. This wasn't the sort of information she wanted. Or needed.

"Hmm… well, thank you."

Polina turned and walked to the stairs. Although they had been rebuilt during the remodeling, each step emitted a slight creak as she made her way to the second floor. The noise had become a constant reminder to everyone that this wasn't a modern hotel with all new amenities, but instead a two-hundred-year-old castle that had been retrofitted to accommodate twentieth-century visitors. The walls on either side of the stairway were lined with numerous black-and-white images of the castle. They were all old photographs, telling a tale of what life was like a century ago. Each one was amazing in its detail and contrast to modern life. No single photographer was credited and the assumption was they had been the work of many different artists. The images had been presented to Razvan by the Romanian government before the hotel opened in recognition for his commitment to showcasing Romania to the world.

Polina reached the top stair and took her first steps into the hallway. She quickly became aware of the Americans, Dan and Isabella, toward the far end of the narrow and rather too-well-lit hall. It was clear they were not getting along, but what she was unable to determine was which of them was drunker. One thing was certain, neither cared that Polina was approaching and was about to bear close witness to their argument. This did, however, bother Polina, who wished the corridor was empty. She wanted to go to her room, take a shower, and relax without having to deal with whatever the situation was Dan and Isabella were involved in.

"Come on," Dan said, "you don't want to be alone tonight, do you?" This was the pathetic plea of a drunk man hoping to score.

"Always the same," Isabella said. "You have one mind and it is both tiny and uninteresting. Not to mention… ineffective."

He moved in closer and placed his hands on her shoulder, almost pinning her to the wall. As Polina closed the gap between her and the Americans, it was becoming quite obvious Dan required the comfort of a woman in his room. What was much clearer was no sane female would ever accommodate his need based on Dan's condition and flirting technique.

"Don't be like that."

Polina was now standing almost opposite them at the door to her room. She was no more than two meters away and the stench of Steel's aftershave blending with an abundance of vodka made her rush to unlock her door. Despite his attempts to seduce Isabella, Dan took the opportunity to eye Polina lecherously.

"Jesus! You can't even flirt without your dick pointing somewhere else," said Isabella. She pushed Dan away and turned to her own room, unlocking the door before she turned back to face him. "Do what I pay you for and find me a role that will win me awards." Isabella stepped into her room and held the door open only wide enough to deliver the remainder of her ultimatum. "Then I'll sleep with you again… perhaps." With those words, she slammed the door on Dan.

Polina was certain this was not the first time he had faced such demands and rejections from Isabella—or for that matter, many women. Without missing a beat, Dan turned to Polina. She smirked in a manner that some may have misinterpreted as flirtatious, but her gesture was far from this. She entered her room and closed the door behind her. Dan was left alone. He shrugged his shoulders and staggered to the door to his own room, number 217. His accommodations were on the same side as Polina's and shared a common wall. He struggled to slide his key into the slot, finding it would not fit. He stared at the key and eyed the lock before realizing he was attempting to insert the key upside down. Another try, and the lock clicked open. His body didn't so much enter the room as fall into it. He kicked the door shut behind him with his foot. The hall was now quiet with the exception of the high-pitched electrical buzz emanating from the overhead lights.

Polina stood inside her room, considering the space. The room was utilitarian at best. A small, tightly made bed, a worn dresser with a tiny black-and-white television, and a round table with a wooden chair were all the room offered its guest. On the far wall, a single window provided a view of the hotel grounds. The only extravagance in the room were heavy floor-to-ceiling drapes lining either side of the opening. The deep-red velvet stood in stark contrast to the drab, dark-green carpet. An unenthusiastic oil painting of a Romanian farmyard with cows and chickens hung above the bed. Polina wondered who chose the paintings that hung in hotel bedrooms. They always invoked a sense of regret rather than one of belonging. Did the hotel's management think their guests would sit and contemplate the goats, ducks, and geese while they prepared for bed? Polina smiled and let out a schoolgirl giggle when she imagined herself staring at the painting while in the throes of sex. When she remembered the last man she slept with, Polina realized the image on the wall would have been the high point of that particular relationship.

She placed her purse on the dresser and laid her small suitcase on the bed. Returning to the bag, she removed a sleek black pistol with an attached suppressor.

Polina checked the gun's preparedness as she walked to the head of the bed and, as she had done dozens if not hundreds of times before, placed the weapon under the pillow with the grip facing toward the edge of the bed, which allowed her to grab the gun correctly and without delay if needed.

Polina popped the two clasps on her suitcase and flipped the lid open. She removed a small black leather portfolio covering a matching set of elegant lingerie and another pair of heels, which she had wrapped individually in cloth, so they would neither get scratched nor catch on any of her delicate clothing. She pulled a perfectly prepared and packed silk suit from under a protective layer of heavy butcher paper, a packing technique she had learned from her grandmother so many years before. Polina took pride in her clothes and would never be caught dead in the subpar quality offered in her hometown. Instead, she preferred the fine wools, silks, and linens found in the more civilized countries to the west. She had often wondered what was holding her back from accepting an assignment in Paris, London, or Milan and not returning upon completion. Stepping out of her heels, Polina set them at the foot of the bed. She removed her nylons with care, not wishing to incur any runs in the fine Parisian material. Reaching back, she unzipped her dress and allowed her finery to fall seductively to the ground. She picked up the garment and placed the expensive silk apparel flat on the bed. A shiver passed through her body as she stood in the room, wearing only a matching set of red underwear and lace bra. Like her boots and purse, Polina had purchased the lingerie at a small boutique in Milan the past summer. She may be a principled Russian, but she was still a woman.

As she walked toward the bathroom, Polina manipulated her hair into a ponytail before twisting the brown locks into a bun, which she secured with a band. Where the bedroom had been spartan and uniquely Iron Curtain in its furnishings, the bathroom reflected a conscientious effort of modernization. The room was spotlessly clean and rather oversized when she compared the space to the many hotel bathrooms she'd been forced to endure throughout eastern Europe. The floor and walls were covered in brilliant white, ceramic square tiles. Each one was no more than three or four centimeters along its edge and Polina began calculating how many squares occupied the space before deciding the exercise was meaningless. A stainless-steel towel rack, gleaming to a high polish, was attached to the wall and held a selection of carefully presented white cotton towels that Razvan had imported from Turkey.

Polina glanced at her image in the mirror and adjusted her breasts in her bra before moving her head from side-to-side to check her face. Using a well-manicured fingernail, she touched up her lipstick in the corner of her mouth, something, in truth, not needing her attention. Her gaze drifted down to the counter where she was pleased by the typical hotel accouterments laid out with absolute precision. The arrangement suggested someone had used a metric ruler to assure the spacing was equal and accurate. Two of the first gifts she remembered receiving from her grandfather were a measuring stick and a compass. He had taught her how to measure and draw circles with the tools and soon she had documented the length of everything in their house. In a moment of quiet thought, she imagined how she missed her *dedushka*, who had always treated her with deep love and affection. She was sure he wouldn't appreciate the employment Polina was now engaged in.

The bathroom counter was white marble, which blended with the walls into one continuous flow of material. Polina reviewed the items sitting before her. She picked up and opened a small container. Closing her eyes, she inhaled the shampoo's aroma and smiled as the citrus scent met with her approval. She screwed the lid back on and returned the bottle to the exact spot it had come from.

A small cylindrical object caught her eye. The receptacle did not bear any label and appeared out of place among the other soaps and lotions. She picked the item up and snapped the top open. A fine string of waxed dental floss stood stiff inside the container. She teased a few centimeters of the floss from the container and cut it with the attached sharp edge. Wrapping the string around her nimble fingers, she pulled the floss between her teeth, moving from front-to-back on one side, then changing to the other side and repeating the process before finishing with her top set. She was an anomaly in Russia as she had no cavities. Her dentist was always surprised at this and perhaps a bit saddened to know he wouldn't be able to drill haphazardly into her beautiful white teeth with—or as was usually the case, without—a shot of Novocain to dull the inevitable.

Polina finished flossing and dropped the string into a trash can positioned under the counter. While flossing was not a revelation to Polina, she did think dental thread was an odd item to find in a hotel. *Interesting,* she thought. *The realities of living under communism are not quite the same in Romania as in the Motherland.* Polina turned around and pulled the clear curtain to the side. The shower-tub combination, in contrast to the whiteness of the room, was a pleasing shade of pink. *Almost a rose color,* she thought. A quick turn of the knob and the room started to fill with warmth and steam.

"My, my, hot water on demand. What would the party say to such extravagance?" For no particular reason, Polina had said this aloud, which was something she wasn't accustomed to doing. Within seconds, the bathroom mirror steamed up and only a faint, unrecognizable reflection of Polina was visible. Polina's ghostly image removed her bra and arranged the undergarment safely on the counter. She slipped out of her underwear and folded them in half, placing them beside the brassiere. Testing the water, she found the temperature to be perfect. Polina stepped into the shower and drew the curtain closed.

Simon King

Chapter 4

By midnight, the raging blizzard had reduced itself to a steady, but far-more-gentle, snowstorm. With each passing hour, it seemed the storm had delivered the last of its snow. The often-unreliable Romanian weather report was proving to be uncannily correct. With the winds now gone, the snow sat heavily on every surface, both horizontal and vertical. The glow of a full moon did its best to cast soft shadows across the mountains and forests. The only other light falling on the grounds of the Hotel Teleki came from the overly-bright lobby area and from a single window high on the hotel's second floor.

Polina's hotel room was pitch black. Her friends in London would say the room was as black as Newgate's knocker, a phrase she never quite understood other than imagining the words must have related to something from another time period. Polina had grown accustomed to sleeping in complete darkness as her father would always complain, "Why pay for having lights on if no one is awake to need them?" As an adult, she had maintained the habit. Her father, physically fit with a drooping mustache, had been a pleasant enough man whose general abstinence from the national drink should have guaranteed he would be a fine dad to his only child and a decent husband to his attractive and kind wife. The endless stress of his job as a homicide detective in Saint Petersburg's central district drove him to bouts of violent anger and, at times, physical abuse directed at Polina's mother. That particular evening in the middle of a summer heatwave, the tension had become too much, and he struck Polina's mother with enough force to knock her across their compact kitchen and into the sharp corner of the dining table. Death had been instantaneous as her head split open and blood drained across the tiled floor. Shocked at what he had done by his own hand, Polina's father put his police pistol into his mouth, and seconds later, Polina was an orphan.

The radioactive glow of an alarm clock was the only light in the room. The device sat on a tiny bedside table next to a tall brass table lamp. All was silent with only the clock's incessant and obnoxiously loud clicking sound as the plastic digits flipped over marking the time during the slow winter night. Polina was deep asleep, but as was her training, she kept one hand under her pillow, her fingers wrapped around her gun. She had been caught unawares once, and she vowed that would never happen again.

A loud crash jolted Polina to a fully upright position. The pistol fell into her grasp naturally and with a single finger, she released the safety, making the weapon deadly in her hands. She glanced at the clock, which glowed with a precise half-past three. Understanding the sound had not come from inside her room, Polina cautiously climbed out of bed. She placed her back against the wall as she crept to the window. She was wearing a short, light pink silk negligee. At home, she slept in the nude, but somehow, it seemed uncomfortable being naked in a bed that was not her own.

The nightie was in stark contrast to the dark black pistol gripped professionally at the end of her dangling but prepared arm. The cold steel of the suppressor touched her bare leg, but she wouldn't allow the resulting goosebumps to interrupt her concentration. Polina's body was an interesting mix of femininity and muscular tone. While some men were unwilling to accept a woman who held her own in a brawl, many women secretly wished they possessed the strength and courage Polina had developed over the years.

Using the barrel of her gun to push one of the drapes aside enough to check outside, Polina used her free hand to wipe a small viewing circle on the steamed-up window. The opening was all she needed to witness the snow still coming down and the shine of the moon reflecting against the brilliant white was sufficient to convince her it was, indeed, the middle of the night. Putting her face close to the casement, she moved her eyes side to side in an effort to understand what might have woken her.

Satisfied the noise did not come from outside, Polina returned her attention to the room. She tiptoed to her door and peered silently through the peephole. The hallway was well lit and she saw her finished meal was still sitting on the floor where she had left the tray many hours before. She had placed the plate and utensils back on the metal platter and put them outside of her door so Otilia, or some other employee, could retrieve the dirty dishes. She was surprised no one had attended to the task yet. Seeing no sign of movement in the hall, she pressed her ear to the door and listened for a moment but again, nothing.

Pulling back from the door, Polina became aware the transparent silk of her nightie offered no barrier to winter's cold, and a shiver passed through her body as goosebumps erupted on her exposed legs. Perhaps it had been a dream? This was, however, a ridiculous assumption as she was not one to be troubled by nightmares. Polina ran the layout of the hallway through her mind and considered where her room was located. On one side, nothing was between her door and the stairs with the exception of a trash receptacle. The walls had been bare, with none of the hotel's memory-inspiring photographs of the way life had been. In the other direction, though, she remembered a door to another room. The digits on the door identified the room as number 217, the room occupied by Dan Steel.

Walking to the dresser, Polina picked up a paper-wrapped drinking glass the resort had provided. As she removed the waxed paper, Polina wondered who had the job of wrapping these glasses. *Sanitized for your protection*, the wrapper always claimed. *Was this true?* she thought to herself. Polina finished unwrapping the vessel as quietly as the paper would allow and placed the glass ever-so-gently against the wall separating her room from Dan's. She leaned across the dresser, pressed her ear to the glass and listened intently for a full minute. *He has the same clock,* she thought and wondered if the painting above his bed was equally mundane. The walls must've been thinner than she imagined, and she was happy Dan had not brought Isabella back to his room for an evening of athletically loud sex.

Again, her investigation provided no details about where the sound had come from. The fact that it was only a single bang, and no further noises followed, seemed strange. Why had no one from the hotel come to investigate? Why hadn't Isabella or Dan in his drunken state opened their door to discover what was going on?

Confused but tired, Polina returned the glass to the table and climbed back into her bed. She pushed her pistol under her pillow and drew the covers tight against her neck. The comfort had already left them and she pulled her legs close to her tummy in an attempt to conserve warmth. Instinctually, she slipped her hand under the pillow, and, once again, grasped her resting gun. Within moments, Polina was asleep and as before, the only sound was the clicking of the clock toward 3:36.

Several hours later, sunlight attempted to part the clouds, turning the snow-covered mountains and the hotel's grounds into a dazzling display of reflections, almost as if millions of diamonds had been dropped from the heavens. The flakes had not stopped falling, but the storm was breathing its last breaths, as the snow had become nothing more than an occasional flurry. Deep snowdrifts in the parking lot assured no one was going to leave Teleki any time soon.

Razvan would tell anyone who asked he had invested heavily in renovating the hotel but no interior space exhibited this expense more than the room with the indoor swimming pool. The finest hotels in London, Paris, and New York did not come close to the opulence created by the master craftsmen responsible for this chamber. To label the luxurious pool as yet another play area was an insult; from the doors and furniture, to the pool itself, not a single Romanian leu had been spared to create a place of wonder and ultimate relaxation.

The room sat at the end of a sloped hallway that started through a door a few steps from the lobby's front desk. Inside the room, a sizable bar occupied one corner where, during the summer months, guests would line up three-deep to order exotic drinks which they consumed slowly while lazing around the crystal blue waters of the oversized pool. More than half of the left wall was taken up by a wood-lined sauna that would comfortably fit twenty oversized guests looking to regain the health and fitness they had somehow lost once they entered middle age.

The pool itself was as beautiful and inviting as any offered by the renowned Hearst Castle in California. But beyond the opulence of the pool, the bar, the sauna, and the Art Deco furnishings, a guest's attention was always immediately captured by the floor-to-ceiling windows covering the entire southern wall of the room. Razvan had hired, once again at great expense, an architectural firm from Milan to engineer the windows, which slid fully open during the warm summer months to allow guests to lounge outside after an invigorating swimming session.

For many, this area, not the pool, was what attracted them. Thin, young women in modern bikinis lay on teak platforms covered by Turkish beach towels in hopes of turning their already tanned bodies into a deeper shade of bronze while their soft, beyond pale, and balding husbands smoked cigars and drank endless glasses of imported Scandinavian vodka. Many of these women were not accompanying a spouse but rather were brought to the resort by wealthy men to peacock to their business associates during the day while providing drunken nighttime entertainment for their sugar daddy back in the privacy of their shared room. Regardless of the time of year and the quality of the guests, no one denied the view out the windows was anything short of spectacular. Rugged mountains shot endlessly skyward and the expanse continued as far as one wished to look down the long sweeping valley to the west.

This morning, as none of the guests had yet to enjoy the pool, the water was still. Not a single ripple was visible. The pool's water appeared frozen in time and exhibited ice-smooth perfection. A curtain of steam rose from the surface tempting anyone who entered the room to break the water's flatness and soak in its warmth. Lilla pushed the room's heavy oak-and-glass doors open and glided in. Her beach sandals slapped against the granite slab floor as she walked and the sound echoed through the space, magnifying in intensity the deeper into the room she advanced.

She wore a thick white cotton robe she had found hanging on the door of her bathroom. The hotel had provided these for guests wishing to walk to the pool without offending others with their flabby bodies paled to china white from too many years behind a desk. On Lilla, the robe was oversized, reaching almost to her feet and hung on her slender frame in such a manner the garment disguised the young body beneath. She picked up a blue towel from a neatly aligned display covering most of a lengthy table and stopped at a stainless-steel chaise lounge near the pool's edge. Lilla threw the towel on the chaise and removed her robe, dropping it on the chair.

At nineteen, Lilla had the type of toned body other girls her age envied. Her flowing auburn hair waved forever in an imaginary wind. The minimal light pink bikini matched her finger and toenail polish perfectly. The high cut thong bottom rested softly on her hips and a matching string top covered only as much of her breasts as necessary. While swimsuits in Hungary and in Russia's satellite countries still carried the unwritten restrictions of conservatism and modesty, Lilla preferred the skimpiest designs offered by the more utopian societies found along the Spanish, Italian, and French Riviera. This particular bikini was straight from the naughtiest beaches of the Mediterranean. She had purchased the two-piece the past summer in the Costa Brava region of Spain while on holiday with her father and Márta.

The trip itself had been enjoyable, but she had secretly longed to sunbathe topless like so many other women on those beautiful beaches. Unable to do this, she settled for the smallest bikini she could find. Her father did not object to the bikini's brevity but had questioned why such a small amount of material had cost so much. However, as Lilla was his only child, and he wanted to spoil her, the purchase was made.

Lilla slipped off her sandals and walked barefoot the last two meters to the pool. She entered its warm waters slowly, taking each step as if she were enticing the cutest boy from her school. Once the water reached her thighs, she dove in. Her entry was the most graceful of arcs and she gave the appearance of being guided by heavenly forces. She swam completely submerged for several meters before her head bobbed above the water's surface. She stopped for a brief moment to smooth her hair back before proceeding to glide with no apparent effort across the pool, extending her arms forward and pushing them outward before drawing them close to her body and repeating the motion. Impossibly, her movement created no extraneous stirring in the almost-still water.

Unbeknownst to Lilla, the door to the opulent room pushed open once again and Alejandro drifted in. It was evident he had not come to swim as he was dressed in the same wrinkled shirt and pants from the night before. Alejandro walked ominously toward the chaise where Lilla had placed her belongings. He picked up her robe and, holding the garment close to his face, breathed in her lingering perfume. Dropping the robe, he picked up the blue towel and continued to the edge of the pool where he stood unfolding the cloth.

Lilla had already reached the far end of the pool and was now finishing her first lap back to where she had started. She swam to the pool's edge where Alejandro's rugged shoes dangled over the coping. Lilla turned her gaze upward and he smiled back at her. This was the sort of smile that melted a girl from the inside. She returned the emotion with satisfaction as a pleasant tremble passed through her body. Without speaking, Lilla made her way toward the pool's stairs. Alejandro walked along the pool's edge, matching Lilla's progress step-for-step. He stopped at its stairs and waited for Lilla to climb out. She took the steps as gracefully as she had done earlier, using all her womanly skills to impress and, more to the point, to tempt.

Lilla had met Alejandro when she was in Spain the previous summer. She had been tanning alone on the beach while her father was in town with Márta. Alejandro had been eyeing her from a distance when he finally summoned the courage to approach her. He wasn't sure how she would react, but he put on his best Spanish machismo tempered with a dash of innocence. Both were happily surprised by the connection they found with each other and arrangements were quickly made to meet every day. Two days later, he had kissed her while they swam in the crystal-clear waters of the Mediterranean Sea. Lilla was heartbroken when she had to return to Hungary, and vowed to make it up to him if they if only they would unite once again.

Months passed, and through a series of clandestine and poorly connected phone conversations, the decision was made they would meet during the winter in Romania.

Lilla took the final step out of the pool and the two came face to face for the first time since their last meeting on the burning sands of Costa Brava. Alejandro's chiseled facial features was at odds with Lilla's dripping and beautiful body. He handed her the towel, which she accepted but did not use. Instead, she allowed the water to drip slowly down her contours.

"You made it," she said. "I wasn't sure this would happen."

"How could I not?" He gently brushed her wet hair behind her ear. Even if she had wanted to, she couldn't halt the deep inhale of breath this action produced. "With an invitation such as you extended," he said, "I would have been a fool to stay away."

Lilla dabbed the moisture from her face and chest with the soft cotton towel. "I was afraid the hotel would be full. Or the storm would keep you from coming."

Alejandro took the towel from Lilla and walked behind her where he began slowly drying the rivulets of wetness from the young woman's back. Rather than rub her dry, he attacked each stream individually, thereby extending the satisfaction both were enjoying. Lilla bit her lip before allowing a smile to explode across her face. Her chest expanded as she breathed in deeply and her eyes journeyed all the way to the right in their sockets, trying to follow Alejandro.

"Those would have been minor inconveniences." He bent down and rubbed the towel slowly along the outside of her upper legs. He pushed the material up the inside of her left leg, stopping short of her bikini bottom before continuing down the other appendage. Her eyes closed as she let out a silent gasp.

"Nothing would have kept me from you."

Whatever he was doing was having the desired effect and Lilla struggled to not spin around and jump into his strong arms. Alejandro stood and walked around to face her again.

"Tell me about the woman you're with."

Lilla's face changed color, and she shook her head in disappointment. *Why bring her up?* she thought. She took a deep breath and shrugged her shoulders.

"Márta. She's my stepmother. This trip was her idea. I mean, I was planning to come alone but when I mentioned the idea to my father, she jumped in and invited herself. I do find it strange, to be honest. I don't know why she would be interested in a quick Romanian holiday in the middle of winter with her stepdaughter. Especially since we more or less hate each other."

"Well, either way, I'm pleased you were able to join her."

Lilla needed to turn the conversation away from Márta, and she quickly calculated how best to accomplish that task.

"I'm going to sit in the sauna for a short bit. You should—I don't know… join me." The words and her accompanying sly smile were irresistible.

"A lovely idea. I would but"—he motioned to his clothing— "as you can tell, I have no swimwear with me."

Once Lilla had set her hooks into something, nothing would stop her. She took Alejandro's hand and guided him toward the sauna.

"As you said, a minor inconvenience."

Lilla pulled the door to the sauna open, letting a wave of uncomfortably hot, wet air escape. She stepped inside and the door closed partially until her Spanish lover stepped in the way.

Alejandro was instantly drenched with the sauna's humid heat. He was fully prepared to join Lilla when he stopped in his tracks. Alejandro perceived a sound—something from across the room perhaps. He was unable to identify what the noise was nor where it had come from, but it bothered him nonetheless. His attention to the disturbance ended as abruptly as it had started. Lilla perched in the sauna's doorway, dangling the bikini top from one hand while she draped her other arm across her breasts, covering them enough but not too much. She flopped the bikini top over Alejandro's shoulder and dropped her other arm to her side. Standing with her left hip thrust ever so slightly to the right, she presented herself in a manner that would have caused a monk to have second thoughts and Alejandro was no monk. Satisfied they were alone and unwilling, or perhaps incapable of ignoring the beauty standing in front of him, Alejandro stepped into the sauna and let the door shut behind him.

The room was now silent with only the sound of chlorinated waves lapping against the sides of the pool. Next to the giant windows, a solitary chaise was positioned to take in the view outside where the snow continued to fall softly. Quietly and with purpose, a pair of long, dark-skinned legs swung from the reclined chair and landed gently on the granite-tiled floor. Anne-Marie stood. Her height was commanding, made even more so by her legs, which were slender but muscular. She was wearing a white bikini with small flower embellishments on each hip and between her breasts. The white suit was in stark contrast to her flawless ebony skin. Anne-Marie grabbed a flowered-knit pareo and wrapped the sheer cloth around her tiny waist—all the while keeping a watchful eye on the sauna across the room. Earlier, she had seen the meeting between Lilla and Alejandro in the reflections of the big windows. She had remained quiet, so as not to interrupt their affair. It was like watching a film and being the only one in the audience. She picked up her coffee cup from a nearby table, took a sip, and thought about what she had witnessed.

"Well now, that was certainly interesting." She said this out loud, as Anne-Marie had no reason to be concerned since she was alone. Anne-Marie gathered her book and towel and left the pool area through the double doors. Behind her, the pool slowly returned to a still-as-ice nature.

Simon King

Chapter 5

The morning started another day for Crina. Her desk always had plenty of paperwork to process, and, today at least, hopes of phone service being reestablished. She was amazed how the loss of such a necessity essentially crippled the Teleki. Regardless, she still had too much to do without constant calls from hopeful tourists requesting a room or canceling a reservation.

Crina had been with the resort for almost two years now, ever since Razvan had posted an advertisement in the Bucharest newspaper seeking a hotel manager. The advert had attracted plenty of responses and Crina considered herself lucky to have landed the job. While she liked to believe Razvan was impressed by her attention to detail and ability to speak several languages, she was also aware he was not offended by her ability to look both professional and attractive in a dress. Crina was bothered by women having such an advantage in life, but she wasn't above utilizing her looks if they advanced her career. That said, she considered herself to be somewhat modest, and she never missed the familial obligation to drop to her knees each evening for prayer. Taking the job had meant leaving her family and everything she had become accustomed to, but working at the resort also provided an opportunity to start over. Life in the city had been an endless series of useless boyfriends whose interest in Crina waned after a few evenings together. She enjoyed the company and the sex was usually satisfactory, but she became aware the men had a different agenda than her own, and she was determined to move on with her life.

"A fine morning to you, miss Crina," said Everett.

His booming voice startled Crina as she was deep in her work and was not aware of him approaching the front desk. Everett was dressed impeccably and Crina wondered why others did not follow his style. Even in her few years, she had seen a dramatic change in how people presented themselves. In the past, men always wore dark suits and ladies would only step outside their home if they were wearing a nice dress and nylons. The men often wore hats and the women would often be seen with a silk scarf. Now, the styles of America had invaded

Romania and Crina witnessed more women in jeans, and the men rarely dressed in an interesting fashion.

"Good morning, Mr. Cook. How may I help you?"

Razvan appeared out of nowhere and rushed to the front desk. He always welcomed the opportunity to meet guests and make an impression on them. Although his English was not up to the high bar set by Crina, he was excited to speak with his guests, especially those as refined as Everett Cook. Crina was sure Razvan had no understanding of the homosexual leanings of Mister Cook. She was certain he would not have approved of such goings-on in the Teleki.

"Hello my sir," Razvan said in his broken English. "You happy today here at my hotel, yes?"

"Absolutely!" said Everett. "You have a fine establishment and a crack set of employees. Running your hotel like a British train schedule, if I may be so bold. As it should be." He tapped his ever-present walking stick against the floor with his last statement as if to add his own punctuation to the sentence.

Razvan was lost by both the speed of delivery of Everett's words and his flourished British idioms. Regardless, he smiled and shook Everett's hand enthusiastically.

"Thank you, Mr. Cook," said Crina. "You will please excuse Mr. Petrescu's English skills. He is still learning the language." Crina always defended her boss in front of guests and was surprised at how much he was able to communicate with his limited vocabulary.

"Of course. Please express my deep satisfaction to Mr. Petrescu. But now, Christian and I are famished." As Everett had grown older, he had become quite set in his ways and one of those was having his meals at specific times each day without delay. Everett used his walking stick to point toward the restaurant. This action made Crina wondered if he really needed the crutch, for he appeared to walk fine without the cane. She decided the stick was more of an accent to his manner of dress and personality. As such, the device was both appropriate and rather dignified. "I presume you have a delicious breakfast being served at this hour."

"Yes, of course!" Crina was always enthusiastic when a guest was polite, as was the case with Everett Cook. Crina arranged her paperwork and straightened her wool skirt before joining the two men on the other side of the counter. "Mr. Petrescu, would you please keep an eye on the front desk while I take these gentlemen to the restaurant?" She didn't need to ask Razvan, but she also was aware he enjoyed seeing her helping his guests and showing them, he was in charge.

"Of course! Enjoy your meal, my guests. We have the finest food in all Romania!" Razvan's broad smile revealed his dark tobacco-stained teeth.

"Please, follow me," said Crina. Crina's heels provided cadence which was matched by Everett's stick as they walked across the shimmering granite floor to the restaurant's doorway.

"By the way," Everett said, "I was awoken by quite a racket coming from the floor above last night. Middle of the night, truth be told. Is everything all right?"

These were the problems Crina faced constantly. From her first days on the job, Razvan set forth the guideline that the guest's comfort and enjoyment must be her top priority so they would either return in person or promote the Teleki to their circle of friends, preferably both. His declaration must have worked because over the years he had spent almost no money on promoting the hotel in newspapers or international travel publications, yet people came from every country in Europe and from all over the United States. He had even had a guest come from Tasmania, although he had no clue where this far away land was.

"I was not aware of a problem," Crina said. "I do apologize and I will look into it right away."

"Please do. Quite difficult to obtain my required time in bed with God-knows-what happening upstairs."

Crina handed the men off to Otilia and returned to the reception desk where Razvan was now speaking with Toma. She wasn't sure what the conversation was about but she was sure that, once again, Toma was unhappy with the demands being placed on him. As she arrived, Toma stormed off toward the hotel's front doors. Crina liked Toma and the two of them had shared a bed on several occasions, but she also understood him to be a bit of a hothead. This had always worried her as she had experience with volatile men in the past and had no interest in going down the same path ever again.

No more than ten seconds after Toma left the desk, loud banging and yelling cascaded down the stairwell, filling the room with endless echoes.

"What the hell is happening?" said Razvan.

Crina imagined the hotel owner's heart doubling its rate and wasted no time to jump into action. She did this both out of personal interest as to what all the commotion was about and to continually prove her value to Razvan. Despite his occasionally gruff demeanor, he was a capable man to work for.

"Don't worry, sir, I shall look into it." She grabbed an oversized walkie-talkie from the front desk and dashed to the stairs. Even in her heels, she was able to take them two at a time and look graceful doing so. She reached the second floor and proceeded briskly down the hallway to the probable cause of the noise: Isabella Manson was pounding incessantly on the door to Dan Steel's room. *Why is it always Americans?* she thought.

"WAKE UP!" Isabella said. "We didn't come all this way so you could get drunk and sleep all day!"

She continued hammering on the door with no concern for others who may still be enjoying their deep slumber. When Isabella had a problem, it was always everyone's problem. More than a few directors and studio heads in Hollywood could attest to this fact. Isabella didn't realize her anger was among the reasons she was no longer securing leading roles in feature films.

Crina quickened her pace and, upon reaching Isabella, jumped into hotel management mode. "Miss Manson, is there a problem? How may I help?"

For whatever reason, Isabella was clearly frustrated and at her wits' end. "Yes… yes, I do have a problem. And yes, you can help. Do you have a key or something? Open this damn door." Despite her anger and the still early hour, Isabella's appearance was flawless. Her appearance made Crina wonder if the actress had stashed a hairdresser and stylist in her luggage.

Crina stepped between Isabella and the door. In the past, she had often been called into duty to calm arguments between guests and this often required placing herself between the warring parties. Typically, the problems were the result of a husband who had drunk too much or a wife who had discovered a dalliance her spouse had been indiscreet with. But this was usually something that occurred in the evening, not at the beginning of a new day.

"I believe you are in the other room, Miss Manson. This room is where—"

Isabella wasn't used to explaining herself. She was angry and she wanted a resolution. And she wanted it now. She eyed Crina with determination, a technique which had served her well in discussion with Hollywood producers who often wished she would move on with being an actress and spend less time complaining about how a certain director was treating her or the touchy-feely hands of a costar.

"I know whose room this is! This is the room of my piece of shit agent. Instead of getting me starring roles, he's drinking and screwing starlets. I don't know what else he does. But I will tell you one thing," Isabella raised her voice toward the door, "IF HE DOESN'T OPEN THIS DAMN DOOR RIGHT NOW, HE'LL LOSE THE BEST ACTRESS HE EVER HAD! YOU HEAR ME, DAN STEEL?" Satisfied Steel could not ignore her outburst and would be, in turn, at least slightly embarrassed, Isabella collected herself and smiled at Crina. "Now, miss—"

Crina had learned to personalize confrontation as working on a first-name basis helped reduce the stress level in such situations. "You may call me Crina."

"All right, Crina. It is imperative this door be opened." Isabella considered her approach to the problem and decided a change in tactics was needed. Time for her hidden charms and years of acting experience to be called into play. "I worry about the health of Dan... of Mr. Steel."

"His health, ma'am?"

"Well, yes. He is—" Isabella pondered her next move. She had to be careful not to go over the top. "He is never late for breakfast. Never. Over-hard eggs, ham, and toast is his favorite meal. The most important one, he always says." Another pause to determine how best to appeal to the young hotel manageress. "I worry he might be... hurt." Isabella smiled inside at her pregnant pause. *Award-worthy,* she thought to herself.

Somewhat convinced, but at the same time aware people would say anything to give themselves the upper hand in difficult negotiations, Crina pulled a passkey from her pocket and faced the door. She tapped on the door lightly but loud enough that any guest inside could not ignore her knocking.

"Mr. Steel, this is Crina, the receptionist. I need to open the door. Do you understand, Mr. Steel? Are you decent?"

Isabella laughed and shook her head gently as she raised her eyes skyward. She pushed her hair back as she spoke. "Dan Steel decent? He hasn't been decent since 1961."

Crina took a deep breath and slid her key into the door's lock. She gave the door one last knock, harder this time as a precaution before turning the key. The door now unlocked, Crina turned the knob gently, careful not to show her trembling hand to Isabella. She had no reason to be nervous as she had done this on numerous occasions before, but something seemed different about today's experience. She pushed the door open a few centimeters but her actions were suddenly stopped by a hinged security lock on the inside barring the door from opening any further. Crina leaned her head into the narrow crevice.

"Mr. Steel? Mr. Steel, this is Crina. I am with the hotel. Are you all right? Can you unlock the door please? I need to speak with you." Crina waited for a second or two, hoping Dan Steel would open the door. "Mr. Steel, it is urgent."

The tap on the door had elicited no response. Not even the slightest indication of any movement one might expect from the rustling of bed sheets or the running of the shower. The only sound to come through the opening was the clicking of the room's alarm clock.

"I knew it. He's probably passed out," said Isabella. She pushed past Crina and yelled into the room. "DAN! DAN! Open the damn door!" She reached an arm inside and waved the appendage about in a useless attempt to unlock the security latch.

Crina stepped away from Isabella to use her walkie-talkie. The situation was escalating, and she now understood this was not going to be a simple case of opening a door. She held the walkie-talkie close to her mouth. "Toma, this is Crina. Can you respond please?"

Outside, Toma was building up a healthy sweat shoveling snow from the parking lot. This was a task he both hated and appreciated. Piling snow into large mounds was his one responsibility where he was free from answering Razvan's nonstop demands for an hour or two but the work was also backbreaking. During the previous winter and this one he had asked Razvan to purchase a tractor with a plow attached but Razvan had screamed at the cost.

"Why would I spend money on machinery when I have a strong maintenance man who can use a shovel to do the same thing?" he had said.

Despite his best efforts the snowfall was winning the battle, but Toma realized giving up would only lead to another argument with his boss. Crina's voice cracked over his walkie-talkie again and he was no longer able to ignore her pleas.

"Toma, are you available?"

Toma pushed the shovel into the snow and unclipped the walkie-talkie from his belt. "Yes, Crina. What do you need?"

Through the two-inch speaker of the walkie, Crina's voice mixed with a healthy dollop of static came in response. "Can you come to the second floor please? We need some help to open a door."

"Is it urgent? Razvan wants me to clear the walkway." He had received these requests before and was aware of what to expect. He would arrive at the door Crina was complaining about and calmly explain she had just not pushed hard enough. A complete waste of his time.

Back on the second floor, Crina shook her head in quiet anger but remained calm. Did he not understand? This was where the two of them often quarreled when they found themselves falling into a personal relationship: he refused to grasp the idea that ultimately, she was his superior at the hotel.

"Yes, please. We have a situation here. Room 217."

"Sure, I'll be right with you."

The reluctance in his voice rang in Crina's ear. She turned to Isabella, who had calmed down a bit once she realized her yelling and pounding wasn't producing the desired result.

"I spoke with our maintenance worker, Toma. He'll be able to help us get into the room."

"Well, I can assure you Dan will have some explaining and apologizing to do. I am so sorry to drag you into this." Isabella produced the smile which had helped launch her career.

"Oh please, this is no problem at all." While not the truth, Crina believed they were the proper words to say at the moment.

The door to room 215 opened and Polina stepped out. She was dressed professionally in a dark blazer and winter skirt. Fine Parisian nylons covered her legs, ending in the additional pair of heels she had packed so lovingly in her suitcase. Her overall appearance was as if she was fresh off the Avenue des Champs-Élysées. Polina was surprised the two women were so close to her door but as was her training, she showed no concern.

"Good morning," Polina said.

"Good morning, Miss Tolkunova," said Crina.

While Isabella jealously admired Polina's heels, she had no time to waste on pleasantries with such a beautiful woman. To her, Polina was the battle she faced at every audition and with every producer. Hollywood was convinced younger was always better, thinner was always better, bigger breasts were always better and if you were young, and skinny, and had large breasts, you were cast regardless of actual acting talent.

In return for the lack of niceties from Isabella, Polina eyed her with a slight look of disapproval. She was friendly with anyone, but acceptance had to be earned.

"What's the problem? Someone was doing quite a bit of banging and yelling this morning."

Her subtle complaint was a jab at Isabella, and she felt it, but showed no emotion in return. Polina pulled her door closed and locked it. The noise produced by the American woman had not awoken her. She always rose early and did forty-five minutes of rigorous exercises. She had been a star athlete in her high school years, breaking many of the school's records for running short and long distances. Polina had also excelled at gymnastics and field events. Staying fit and nimble was what set her apart from other women in her business.

"I'm so sorry for the disturbance," said Crina. "Yes, we've had some difficulty with this room, but we'll have the situation straightened out soon. They are serving breakfast downstairs if you wish to join them."

Polina understood the manager's job included not involving one hotel guest in another's problems, but she was not particularly concerned with food at the moment. She recalled the events of the night before and her inability to identify what had caused the sound and from where it had come from. These problems continued to nag at her in the morning while she dressed and brushed her teeth.

"Last night, or perhaps I should say this morning... yes, at three-thirty this morning, I was startled by quite a loud bang and I do believe the sound came from this room." Polina again examined Isabella, her Russian eyes drilling into the American. "This is your friend's room, is it not? Dan Steel, I believe. Am I correct?" This time, rather than offer a supportive smile, Polina allowed no emotion to give any clue as to why she was asking such pointed questions.

An odd mixture of confusion and a hint of jealousy came to Isabella. Women like Polina— and the list was long—always had their nose in business miles beyond their neighborhood. They always had too much knowledge or at least professed to knowing more than they should.

"Yes, this is Dan's room. How do you know his name? Do you two know each other?" Isabella recalled how she had left her agent outside her room last night and how Polina was still in the hall when she closed her door. Perhaps Polina had done for Dan what she would not.

Crina was relieved when Toma arrived at the top of the stairs. She sensed the rising tension between Polina and Isabella and feared she might soon have a second issue on her hands. Dealing with a locked room was one thing, refereeing a battle between two women was quite another.

Toma carried his canvas bag full of tools. As he walked, the various hammers, screwdrivers, and wrenches made an ungodly noise so early in the morning and Crina was happy when he came next to her and silenced the tote by placing the bag on the ground.

"Hi, Crina. What's the problem?"

She pushed the door open again to show it was locked from the inside. "The guest in this room isn't responding, but the security lock is set, so we can't enter. Do you know of a way to open the door?"

"From here, no, opening the door cannot be done. But if I can go through one of the other rooms on this side, I might be able to open the window to this room and go inside and unlock the door."

"I see. Unfortunately, all the rooms on this floor are occupied by other guests. I'll need to ask."

Polina wasted no time in taking advantage of the situation. "You may go through my room if that will help."

"Oh, please, Miss Tolkunova, you aren't under any obligation to do that."

Jumping at the opportunity being presented, Isabella dropped her outward distaste for Polina. Her many years as an actress had taught her to change her emotions almost magically. "Actually, that would be wonderful. Quite helpful. That is, if you don't mind?"

"Of course, no problem at all. Here, let me open my door." Polina smiled. *This stupid American knows nothing of my reasons for wanting access to Dan Steel's room,* she thought.

Polina returned to her own door and unlocked it. She entered, followed by Crina, Toma, and finally, Isabella. She had made her bed and her belongings were put away. Everything was orderly. The room appeared as if no one had slept in it last night. As a child, Polina's mother had insisted she made her bed every morning and kept her room neat in case they had visitors, which they never did. Like sleeping in the dark, this was another trait she carried with her into adulthood. Polina stepped to the side to allow Toma to pass, all the while keeping a distrustful eye on Isabella as the actress moved into her private space.

Toma made a beeline for the window. Polina had opened the drapes earlier in the morning to fill the room with filtered sunlight while she did her calisthenics. Setting down his noisy tool bag once again, Toma opened the window and leaned outside looking toward Dan's window. He pulled his head back in and turned to Crina.

"Yes, I can make this work. Of course, if the window of the other room is locked, I'll need to do something more drastic." He reached into his tool bag and retrieved a long, slender screwdriver. He held the tool up for the women to see, smiling as if the implement gave him some divine power. "Just in case," he said before pushing the pointed tool deep into the rear pocket of his pants.

"Please, if you can," said Isabella. She flashed a smile at him, as if her twinkling lips were a magic charm. For too many men, that was the case.

"Toma, do your best," said Crina.

As Toma bent to move his tool bag out of the way, Crina stepped past him to look out the window.

"Toma! This ledge is tiny and covered in snow! I can't let you do this. We'll find another way. We must!"

Too late. Toma pushed Crina aside and climbed through the window. He sat on the windowsill with the heels of his work boots perched on a narrow ledge. The architectural feature ran the full circumference of the hotel at this height. The sill was no more than twenty centimeters wide and outwardly sloped, but once he brushed away the collected snow, the ledge offered sufficient footing. With white flakes still falling, Toma turned to face inward and held onto the bottom edge of the window's casing in Polina's room. He slid his right foot forward, brushing the snow from the ledge as he advanced. Fortunately, the snow in Romania was rather dry and no ice had formed under the powdery layer of white. Toma moved his left hand to the extreme end of Polina's window sill and started to counterbalance his weight on the protrusion. He remembered from experience that the distance between the two windows was too great to reach from one to the next.

Having advanced his body as far forward as possible, Toma faced a gymnastic dilemma. Relying on his forward-most foot for stability, he raised his other leg toward Polina's open window to counterbalance his body. Moving ever so slowly, he leaned his upper body across the featureless space between the windows. If one were watching his actions from below, Toma would have appeared to be a ballet dancer. His movements were delicate and well-rehearsed. The tips of his finger finally touched the edge of Dan's window. He inched further forward and as he was wrapping his fingers around an opportune edge on the window sill to Dan's room, Toma's right foot gave out with a dramatic slip. This was followed by the little grip he still had on Polina's window flying loose. His body swung wildly from his only handhold on Dan's window while his legs banged painfully against the narrow ledge, knocking masses of snow to the ground far below.

Struggling against gravity, Toma pulled himself upward with one arm and grabbed the window with his second hand before regaining his footing. He breathed deeply, knowing this event might have ended badly. After living through war and facing the difficulties of daily life in prison, to die while attempting to open a hotel guest's locked room was not something he wished to consider. With one hand grasping the window trim, Toma used the other to test the window.

"Shit!"

As he feared, the window was locked. He withdrew the screwdriver from his pocket and wiggled the tool into the crack between the window and its casement. He had done this on several other occasions, but always from a ladder and always during the summer months, so he had prior knowledge in positioning the tool so as to be most effective. With a slow twist, the lock popped and the window swung open.

Wasting no time, Toma climbed in and secured the window behind him. He brushed the snow off his pants and stomped his boots before returning the screwdriver to his back pocket. Only then, did he look up and examine the room. The athletic body of Dan Steel was sprawled facedown on the floor in the narrow space between the bed and the dresser. Other than his swimsuit, Steel was naked and the gray-white pallor of death was obvious. The distinct odor of death had begun to fill the room and Toma wondered why they had not smelled his putrefying body from the hallway.

He stood for a moment, considering the situation. As a small child, he had seen plenty of dead people, but each of those was in the context of the ruins of war. He had seen death again while serving as a young man in the Romanian army. But this was different. This was not a soldier's body on the battlefield, but a guest in the comfort of a hotel bedroom. He quickly realized this particular death appeared dramatically odd; no apparent blood or signs of violence were to be seen on the body. The scene in front of him was almost clinical in nature.

Crina and Polina had moved from Polina's room and now waited anxiously in the hallway for Toma to open the door to Dan's room. Isabella stood by too, but she was decidedly less patient than the other women. She would not stop rapping her fingers against his door as if the resulting noise would somehow drive Toma to act more swiftly. In reality, he paid no attention to her scratching and all her actions did was put Crina on edge.

After what seemed to be far too long, Toma approached the door and, a moment later, he pushed it closed from inside. The squeak of the security lock being disabled was followed by the door opening. Toma cracked the door open only enough to address the women standing in the hallway and no more. As he opened the door a bit more, he strategically positioned himself to block any view which would reveal the dead body of Dan Steel.

His face was solemn and Crina realized he was about to announce something none of them were ready for.

"Crina,"—he swallowed before continuing— "perhaps we should ask the other women to leave."

"What's wrong, Toma?"

Toma peered through the gap in the doorway at Isabella and Polina before returning his gaze to Crina. Toma had a look in his eyes Crina had not seen before. Something not pleasant. Over the past two years, she had worked with Toma on a daily basis and had encountered his many moods. In addition, the sexual dalliances the two of them had had been enjoyable at the time, but she always regretted them later. Today, Crina experienced something new and uncomfortable in his person, and it was not something she liked.

"The man, in this room... He is dead."

Polina pushed forward to face Toma. "Dead?" She asked. "Are you sure?"

Crina and Toma were surprised by Polina's unflinching interest in a dead man she was not familiar with. Individually, they both began to question who Polina was and why she had chosen to stay at the hotel at this time.

Isabella eyes bulged as the conversation sunk in.

"Did..." Isabella said. "Did you say, dead? That can't... That can't be." The straightness of her posture was visibly failing and her knees appeared ready to give up the little support they offered.

Crina did her best to take charge. This would be, she was certain, the first death in the hotel's history. Razvan would not be pleased, that much was obvious.

"Miss Manson, I'm sure this must be a mistake. Perhaps you should wait here for a moment."

Taking advantage of the confusion, Polina pushed Dan's door open and walked past Toma into the room. Toma was surprised such a thin woman would be able to break the hold he had on the door with complete ease. She stood a few meters from Dan's body and examined the scene. For her, the room and those standing nearby were silenced and frozen as she took in every aspect of the crime.

And this was a crime. She had immediately determined that and held no doubt or debate about that in her mind. Coupled with his confusion at seeing her breeze past him, Toma was also quietly confused by Polina's total lack of shock or horror. He had never seen this in a woman before. But this was not the first dead body Polina had found herself examining. Over the recent decade, Polina had come into contact with plenty of dead or dying individuals; some of them fresh with their last breaths still hanging in the air and others in various states of decay.

Since the door was open and Toma had made no move to keep her out, Isabella entered and the sight of the body hit her gut like the unexpected return of a boomerang. She fell to the ground screaming, covering her face briefly before glancing at Dan's corpse and then burying her head in her hands again. Unlike Polina, this was the first dead person she had ever laid eyes on. Of course, she had worked with actors playing dead and that, too, had brought her shivers, but acting in a scene with someone pretending to be dead was nothing compared to the actual corpse laying on the floor in front of her. And not only was this the body of a dead man, but also the body of a man she had worked with for many years, someone she had shared numerous nights of deep passion with.

Crina, too, was shocked at the scene she witnessed, but she contained her outward emotions. She knelt beside Isabella, attempting to comfort her, knowing this compassion and empathy probably meant nothing to her at this time. Crina was not foreign to death, having come upon a gruesome car crash only a year before. She had driven to Bucharest to be with her parents for the weekend and was returning to the hotel late in the evening during a steady rain. She rounded a long dramatic switchback in the road only to come across a car engulfed in flames, and wrapped around a sturdy tree at the road's edge. As she came to a stop, the car's passenger climbed through a window and staggered, like a walking flame, down the highway toward Crina. The young woman was only meters from Crina's car when she fell on the road, convulsed for a moment, and then died. At the same instant, the flames must have reached the vehicle's gas tank because a gigantic explosion lit up the night. As the ball of red and orange settled, Crina saw the driver's dead body, his hands melting into the plastic of the steering wheel. The memory of that evening had come to her in nightmares for many months after.

Without taking her eyes off Dan's body, Polina said, "Toma, correct?"

"Me? Yes, that's correct."

Polina scanned the room. Something was wrong, a bit off. She was unable to immediately tell what the anomaly was, but her training told her not all was as it should be. *What was it?* she thought.

"Toma, have you touched anything in this room?"

"No ma'am." Toma pointed to the window. A distinct puddle remained where the warmth of the room had melted the snow he had brushed from his clothes. "I climbed in the window, looked at the body, and stepped over him to open the door." He paused for a moment before adding, "But I touched... nothing. Nothing else." He glanced down at Dan's body. "He's dead, right?"

Polina ignored his inquiry. *Is that not obvious?* she thought, wondering why he had bothered to ask such a question. Satisfied nothing near the body concerned her, she moved closer and stepped over Dan's corpse to consider his body from a new vantage point.

Crina was alarmed watching Polina move about Dan's body so calmly. *Why is she not upset at this sight?* Crina thought. She was becoming more and more convinced it was wrong for Polina, who appeared to be no more than a routine hotel guest, to be so interested and apparently unmoved by what the four of them were facing.

"Miss Tolkunova, please, we must wait for the police." This was all she could say without losing the tiny amount of calm she still possessed.

"Polina. Please, call me Polina." She had said this without catching sight of Crina. She had anticipated this suggestion and was actually a bit surprised the hotel manager had not said something sooner.

Polina was in her own world as she reached down to put her fingers on Dan's neck. No pulse, which wasn't surprising to her but, but her training told her the check was required. She was about to move her attention elsewhere when something caught her eye. Up high behind his left ear. *What is that?* she thought. Polina leaned in and examined the area closely. She ran her fingers over Dan's skin, pausing momentarily to consider what she was seeing. A single drop of coagulated blood rested below a tiny puncture wound, no bigger than a millimeter in diameter. Rather than alert the others to her find, Polina let her eyes trail the length of Dan's body checking for anything else out of the ordinary. She placed her hand on his swimsuit. His trunks were dripping wet and a lingering odor of chlorine filled the air near his body. The carpet under his body was also wet with chlorinated water.

"Did he fall?" Toma said. "Did he hit his head? Why is there no blood?"

"Well," Polina said, "he did indeed fall. That would account for the loud noise last night. That, and the morbidity of the body, puts his death close to 3:30 this morning, which is when I was awoken by the sound." She was aware of more than these simple facts, but she had no reason to involve civilians in her findings.

Polina stood and again examined the floor surrounding the body. Nothing out of place and no signs of a struggle. She inspected the room. The bed was made and had not been slept in; the covers bore no indication of that. Instead, the bed was presented in the condition a guest would expect when they first entered their room. Dan's clothes were tossed onto the bed as only a man, especially one who had consumed too much alcohol might do. Spotting his open suitcase on the floor next to his bed, Polina went to the travel case and examined the minimal contents inside. Absolutely nothing of interest other than enough wrapped condoms to satisfy several long weekends away from home. A blue towel hanging from the far edge of the bed caught Polina's eye. She picked the towel up. As she did, a room key with the attached fob fell to the floor. The key was identified as belonging to room number 217.

"That is a pool towel," said Crina.

"Are you sure?"

"Yes, our room towels are white and the pool towels are blue. We keep a supply of them in the pool area."

Polina moved back to Dan's body and covered his head and upper body with the towel.

"No blood loss and no bruising," she said to no one in particular. "I believe he was already dead before he fell."

This clinical pronouncement was too much for Isabella, and she ran from the room. Seconds later the slamming of the door to the actress' room echoed through the hallway.

Crina was sure the noise had traveled to the farthest corners of the expansive hotel. With Isabella gone, Crina was now free to deal more effectively with Polina.

"How can you be so sure? Are you a doctor? A policewoman? I don't understand." Razvan was going to demand answers when she told him about the murder so the more information she had, the easier to control his outburst of anger.

For now, Polina had no time for these or any other questions. She wasn't trying to be rude to Crina, but the manager's quizzing did nothing to help put together the puzzle of Steel's death. The time would come for Polina to address Crina's concerns, but that time was not now.

"Toma," Polina said, "when you climbed across, was the ledge covered in snow?"

"Yes. I had to kick the snow off." Toma indicated the movements with his leg. "To move along, you understand."

"And was the window unlocked?"

Toma pulled the screwdriver from his back pocket. "No. The window was locked. But I opened it with this. I've had to do this before. With other windows, I mean. Sometimes people slam their doors closed when they leave the room and the security locks will swing across, making it impossible to open the door from the outside. When that happens, I must climb up a ladder, go through the window, and open the door like I did today."

Polina accepted his explanation as reasonable. She walked past Crina and Toma toward Dan's door and then closed it to examine the security locking system. Polina swung the mechanism back and forth from its locked position to an unlocked position several times.

The latch moved quite easily so it was within reason to imagine this might happen to someone, as Toma said, and they would find themselves needing to call management to solve the problem. As she positioned the security device back to its unlocked state one last time, her eyes were drawn to the peephole in the center of the door. The hole was similar to the one in her room, but this one was unfinished. She rubbed her finger over the coarse hole and placed her eye against the opening. As the hole lacked the fisheye-lens part of the brass cylinder, the view was less useful than the one offered in her own room. She pulled back and questioned Toma.

"Why is the door like this?"

Toma came to where Polina stood. He placed the tip of his finger in the tiny opening. "I am putting peephole devices in each door. For security. I drilled all the doors in this hall yesterday, but I didn't have enough peepholes to finish this door." Apprehensive and somewhat self-conscious, Toma pulled his finger away from the hole and shoved his hands into his pockets. "All the others were finished. All, except this one. I needed another part and planned to complete the job this afternoon. I'm sorry." He felt foolish for apologizing. The guy's death was not his fault, and he was sure his murder had nothing to do with an unfinished peephole.

Satisfied once again with his explanation, Polina walked into the bathroom. Crina's concern was growing as she followed her.

"Please, I don't think this is right. We must... What do they say?"

"Preserve the crime scene," said Polina. Crina was beginning to annoy her, so she decided she needed to at least entertain her latest question.

"Yes. Yes, that is it! We must wait for the police. And a doctor. Please, I insist."

Polina was listening but her eyes were busy with the room. Dan's bathroom was a mirror image of her own. Like the bed, the washroom had not been disturbed, with the precisely folded towels hanging on the rack as the maid would have placed them. The floor towel to be used while bathing was still neatly folded over the edge of the bathtub as had been the case in her own room. She turned to Crina and spoke calmly, using a technique she had been taught and perfected over the years.

"I appreciate your concern." Polina reached for Crina's hand and held it gently in her own. "For the moment, we don't have a doctor nor a policeman. I have some skills that will help you when the time comes, but for now, I must be allowed to do this on my own. Please understand." She squeezed Crina's hand with enough force to show she cared but also to remind her she should be left alone to do her work.

The words and Polina's hand-holding succeeded in calming Crina, as Polina knew they would. She held her hand for a moment longer as she smiled at the hotel manager. Polina recognized this might not be easy for the young woman as sudden death was never easy for untrained civilians to cope with. She also recognized any crime scene investigation became less credible the more time passed and the last thing she needed at this moment was a group of incompetent policemen wrapping the room with plastic warning tape as they trampled the site and chased useful witnesses away.

Polina returned to her examination of the bathroom. No personal effects were on the counter: no toothbrush, no comb, no shaving kit. Nothing. Polina wondered how much time Dan spent in his room and what, if anything, he had done while there. She recalled not hearing him after she left him alone in the hall the night before. Perhaps he had opened his door to leave an hour or two later, but she could not be sure. Something was not quite right about the puncture wound she had seen on his body, and she was equally troubled as she examined the bathroom. At first, Polina thought perhaps she was being overly cautious and, she should accept the murder of Dan Steel as an inconvenience and move on, letting the police and medical professionals work the case. As she took steps to leave the lavatory, Polina absentmindedly surveyed the countertop. Something stood out: one detail, one discrepancy, that made no sense in an otherwise sterile environment.

"Are you familiar with the items the cleaning woman puts in the bathroom?"

"On the counter, yes. We supply two bars of soap, small bottles of shampoo and conditioner, and a container of dental floss."

Polina picked up the shampoo bottle. "In each room?"

"Yes. Every room has the same items."

"Then where"—Polina returned the container to its exact location and spun the bottle carefully until the label faced forward— "is the dental floss for this room?"

Crina was confused by the question. She wondered why Polina was addressing such trivial matters while a dead man was sprawled across the floor in the other room. Surely, Dan Steel's corpse must have been of greater importance than a complaint about missing dental floss. She scanned the bathroom counter for clarification.

"I don't understand. The maid always places the same items in each room. Perhaps she ran out. I shall check with her." Crina went into the bedroom to use her walkie-talkie. Upon seeing Dan Steel's legs protruding from the blue towel, she reconsidered and opened the door to step into the hallway.

Polina followed Crina into the hall. She closed the room door behind her, wondering how long until Toma became uncomfortable being alone with Dan's body and joined them in the hall.

Sooner than she imagined, the door swung open and a rather pale-looking Toma sprinted out, holding his tool bag.

"Do you need me anymore? I have some other jobs I must attend to." Polina was sure she saw beads of sweat on his forehead.

"No, that's fine. Thanks for your help here today. I can find you in the hotel if I need you, right?"

"Yes, I never leave." He appeared to bow to Polina a little before turning away and dashing to the stairs.

Polina smiled. *Even strong men are uncomfortable when left alone with death*, she thought.

She again closed the door to Dan's room and placed her eye close to where the peephole pierced the door. Some thin white threads clung to the hole where Toma had drilled, but not sanded, the opening. Polina pulled on the tiny strands, which were no more than a centimeter in length. She rubbed the strings between her fingers experiencing as she did a waxiness. Holding them to her nose, she identified the distinct odor of mint. As she did this, she became aware Crina was standing nearby, awaiting her attention.

"The maid says she is positive she supplied this room with dental floss. She assures me every room on the floor was cleaned and supplied before the guests arrived. She has been doing this job for several years, and she is excellent at her work. I have no reason to doubt her."

Polina nodded her approval before turning away and moving in painfully slow steps down to the far end of the hallway. She stayed close to the right wall as she walked and her eyes remained focused on the floor during the entire journey. Polina sensed Crina eyeing her with confusion, but this was of no interest to her. She had no need to explain what she was doing or why.

Reaching the end, Polina turned and walked along the other side of the hall, this time staying close to the other wall but still staring only at the floor as she inched forward. As Polina passed Isabella's room, the actress opened her door and stepped out to monitor the process. Polina was certain the American had wanted to say something, but she was grateful she had decided to stay silent.

Both Isabella and Crina saw no rhyme or reason in whatever Polina was doing and to them, her actions were a waste of precious time.

Polina returned to where Crina was standing but then continued past her toward the stairway. She reached the top of the stairs and paused for a brief moment to peer down them toward the lobby before walking back in Crina's direction. Polina stopped at the slender ashtray resting along the wall shy of where Crina waited. The cigarette Razvan had stubbed out in the ashtray yesterday still rested in the smooth chrome bowl. Near the top of the tube, perhaps a third of the way down, was an elliptical opening. The hole was for garbage that had no place being thrown into the ashtray. Polina bent down and appraised the dark hole. Something inside caught her eye. She lifted the ashtray and placed the bowl on the ground. She examined the length of the tube. Polina removed a small pink handkerchief from her jacket pocket and reached deep into the apparently empty trash can. She wrapped the cloth around something small and withdrew the object for closer examination in the light of the hallway. Resting in the folds of Polina's handkerchief was a white cylinder of dental floss.

Chapter 6

Razvan is at the front desk, doing his best to speak with Lilla and Márta. They are asking detailed and difficult questions, that, to Razvan, were arriving at the speed of a Russian rocket. He smiled and delivered answers in hopes they might be what the women were expecting, but their expressions told him he was failing miserably. He recalled Crina's warning that he must learn to speak English more fluently to be able to effectively help the guests. Razvan hated to admit he was wrong, but she was right.

Crina stepped from the stairs and crossed the lobby at what seemed to Razvan to be a run. Polina followed patiently and several steps behind, appearing lost, was Isabella. No one would have believed they were all witnesses to the same situation upstairs as they appeared in to be in completely different moods.

"Crina, excellent. You are here. I think these ladies have a question, but I do not understand what they are asking." At that moment, his employee's frenzied state and the faces of concern on Polina and Isabella came to his attention. His own worry and confusion now doubled as he hoped she would not be bringing him more troubles. "What is happening? What is all this commotion?" Razvan absentmindedly reached into his pocket for a cigarette. He had no intention of smoking in front of guests, but caressing the silver case between his fingers brought him a sense of calm.

Crina pulled him aside and spoke quietly. "One of the guests has died. We must call the police." She regretted telling her boss so abruptly, as his response was less subtle and Márta and Lilla's ears perked up.

"WHAT! Who? In my hotel?" Realizing his amplitude may cause an issue with those present, Razvan quickly regained his composure. "Did he drown in the pool? How did it happen?"

Crina ignored his questions and moved to the desk, where she picked up the phone. Her hands were visibly trembling and her breath was shallow as she dialed. A mixture of fear, confusion, and resignation crossed her face as she listened to the silence coming through the phone and remembered the lack of service. She held the receiver in her shaking hands. She was near her wits' end.

"What do we do? What am I to do?" she said to no one in particular.

Toma was standing nearby, waiting to talk to Razvan. He came to Crina and faced the wall, so the guests would not hear his quiet voice.

"The body. We must do something about the body."

"What? What should we do? What do we do with a"—she lowered her voice— "with a dead body?"

Polina sensed the situation deteriorating rapidly. Crina was not going to be much use unless guided in her decisions and actions. She joined the two hotel workers at the desk.

"Toma," Polina said, "can you find another strong man to help you move the body?"

Crina jumped at Polina's question.

"Move the body? Where? This is a resort, not a morgue. We aren't exactly set up to deal with dead bodies." Crina's eyes bulged as she spoke.

"We need to keep him cold. You don't want a decomposing body stinking up the hotel, do you?"

These words were, of course, a bit dramatic, but Polina believed her bold phrasing necessary to keep the young hotel manager on her toes and focused on the task at hand. Moreover, Polina needed Crina mentally stable if she was going to unwrap the mystery of Dan Steel's death. She ignored Crina to address Toma, who at least had the right idea.

"Toma, does the Teleki have an unheated storage area outside? Somewhere quite cold?"

111

"Yes. We have a small tool shed out behind the hotel. I can take the body to the shed." He turned to Crina. "I will have Ilam help me. Perhaps you can keep the lobby clear of guests when we move Mister Steel. I don't think it would be smart to have anyone else see us walking through with his body."

Crina was regaining her composure and coming around to the plan.

"Yes. Excellent idea. But wrap him in a tarp or something to disguise what you are carrying. Razvan and I will keep people in the restaurant. Call me when you are ready to come down with..." Crina closed her eyes for a brief moment to find her strength. "The body."

The plan conceived and approved, Toma went to the kitchen to find Ilam. The two men did not always get along, but Toma was hoping, for once, the chef would not complain about what needed to be done. Crina straightened her jacket and ran her sweaty palms down her skirt. She pasted on her biggest smile and turned to face Márta and Lilla at the front desk.

Polina now had to start asking the right questions of the right people. First on her list was Isabella. Nothing could hide the American's nervousness and confusion as Polina came toward her. This was not a case of her superior acting skills carrying a fictional character. This was real life, and Isabella was not pleased to be in a position where she had no idea what to do, what to say, or what to think. The circumstances were as foreign as Romania itself.

"How do you do it?" Isabella said to Polina. The words tumbled from her mouth like loose bricks from a wall.

Aware she needed everyone on her side, Polina comforted the woman. While she doubted the actress had the skill to carry out such a perfect murder, she recognized Isabella had a strained relationship with her manager, and describing their situation in this manner was being generous. *For what reason would someone kill Steel?* Polina thought. Perhaps Isabella may have a lead that would point her in the right direction.

"I understand this is difficult. I do. But I am familiar with situations like this. Events like this are part of my training."

"The receptionist, Crina, she asked you if you are with the police. Are you? Are you a policewoman?"

Polina needed to dance around the question. The complete and truthful answer would only lead to trickier questions she had no desire to address.

"I'm trained in forensics. I am aware of what needs to be done under these circumstances." This was a true enough statement, although Polina understood the response might not directly satisfy Isabella's need for a fully truthful answer. However, this did not seem to matter, for Isabella had found some comfort in her words. "Perhaps Crina can find us a place to talk for a moment. Someplace quiet. Please wait here, I'll ask."

Polina left to speak with the Crina while Isabella wrung her hands. A mass of saliva slid down her throat, and she had the guilty thought she would now have to

113

find a new agent, which was not going to be an easy task considering her reduced status in the industry.

"Does the hotel have a quiet room where I can talk with Isabella?" asked Polina. "She needs some comforting and I think I can calm her down a bit."

Having successfully moved Lilla and her stepmother to the restaurant for breakfast and always wanting to please, Crina jumped into management mode.

"Yes, of course. We have a library down the hall. I'll take you to it." Crina leaned toward her boss. "Razvan, I need to show these guests to the library. I will be right back."

The library's massive oak-and-glass entryway was almost identical to those guarding the pool area. They swung heavily as Crina pushed them open. Although entry to the room only required the opening of a single door, she always opened both to show off the room's grandeur. Crina walked in to present the room followed closely by Polina, who held Isabella's hand.

A wall of floor-to-ceiling windows flooded the space with natural light, illuminating an enormous chandelier hanging from the ornately embellished ceiling rather superfluously. Two other walls were lined with bookshelves packed with books. Between each bookcase were large black-and-white photographs of hunting scenes and above those were the taxidermized heads of various animals, none of which were native to Romania. At the far end of the oversized room, a display case with a collection of ancient daggers stood next to a large stone fireplace. A fire was already burning loudly, heating the room to a comfy temperature while also filling the space with the pleasant aroma only a wood-burning fire delivered. Above the mantle hung a landscape painting reflecting a peaceful summer scene in the Romanian mountains. Overall, the decorations were an eclectic collection of violence, death, murderous implements, all culminating in a tranquil pastel and a wonderful assortment of literature.

The library was furnished with inviting couches and several comfy chairs, each with a nearby small table. A long oak table with numerous hard-backed chairs occupied the center of the room and an ancient grandfather clock ticked punctually and audibly from near the doorway. The clock's dark-walnut finish provided an air of legality to a place intended for personal escape and relaxation. This was especially true if the guest was a bibliophile.

"Will this do?"

Polina had expected something smaller and less ominous. "Absolutely. Thank you." She was not sure if the room would be intimate enough to settle Isabella, but Polina would do her best with what she was given.

Polina need not have worried. Isabella floated through the room, as if on a film set. She moved quietly past one of the bookcases and allowed her fingers to drift across the titles. The mass of books calmed her. As an actress, she had read hundreds of scripts and most of them had been horrid. They all painted the lead woman as nothing more than eye candy for the leading man. Lately, as the censors had relaxed, the screenplays contained more and more violence and the sex scenes had begun to border on pornographic. Isabella did not consider herself to be prudish, but she was always more interested in the script's story and overall character development—something actors referred to as their arc—rather than satisfying the ego and sexual deviances of the director or the bean counters tucked away in luxurious studio offices.

When scripts failed her, she found escape in the magical adventures that literature painted for her. The works of the great American and European writers created worlds she imagined herself acting in or, given the opportunity, living in. Hemingway, Fitzgerald, Orwell, Camus, Tolstoy, Nabokov… these were names she turned to for salvation from the crazy, unreal world of Hollywood.

"Would you ladies like anything?" said Crina. She wanted to stay and see how Polina worked while also making sure she did not offend Isabella when she questioned her.

Isabella's distraction from the ominous event upstairs ended, and she perked up at the suggestion.

"What do you think, too early to have a glass of wine?"

Crina visually checked Polina for approval. She did not need to do this, but making sure Polina agreed with the request was somehow appropriate. Polina gave a silent nod.

While she had no intention of dulling Isabella's senses with alcohol, Polina believed a glass or two might help her provide the answers she needed and, at a pace that would solve the case much sooner.

"Not at all. I shall ask Otilia to bring something." Crina left the library and closed the doors behind her. She paused outside to stare through the window back into the room. Alone, Crina was calm, if not stronger in appearance.

Polina wondered if perhaps the manager's early shock and confusion had come from a different place. Polina was aware Crina was standing behind the door, studying the two of them. This behavior caused her some concern; perhaps the manager knew something about Dan Steel or about his death that would help solve the unanswered questions bouncing around the mystery. Polina realized everyone in the hotel, the guests, and the staff, must not be considered above suspicion.

She turned her attention back to Isabella, who had pulled a thick tome from one of the shelves. The cover of the book was coated in dust and the floating particles made a transparent cloud in the air as she thumbed through the pages, stopping occasionally to read a passage before continuing to work her way through the book. *What is this woman hiding?* Polina thought.

"Isabella, perhaps you would like to sit with me?"

Polina's words broke Isabella's trance. She closed the book and placed it gently on the shelf, exactly where the tome had lived previously. While a casual reader may have put the book back and left it at that, Isabella slid the title into place and pulled the book back ever so slightly so its spine aligned perfectly with others on the shelf. A final quiet reflection as her hand rested on the book and she was ready to face Polina. Isabella gathered her wits, straightened her silk-flowered dress, and unnecessarily fluffed her flowing hair before walking to where Polina was standing.

"I wish I had your strength," Isabella said.

Polina indicated two deep-purple chairs with a small round table resting between them. "Please."

As the women settled into the chairs, Otilia knocked on the door. With no need to ask permission, Otilia entered. Held high on an extended hand was a silver tray with a tall bottle of wine and two glasses. Sitting on a brightly-colored plate in the middle of the platter was a small collection of tiny pastries.

"Excuse me, Crina asked me to bring you some wine."

"Yes, of course. Thank you," said Polina.

Otilia came to the two women and carefully removed the glasses and bottle from the platter and arranged them on the table. "Our chef put together a few pastries for you. These are *Papanasi*. They are a delicious traditional Romanian breakfast pastry." She placed the plate of baked goods in the center of the small table.

Isabella took a deep breath and smiled. Polina noted the smile provided an excellent start for the questions to follow.

"No reason to begin my diet today," said Isabella.

The moaning about one's weight or the growing sag of flesh under an actresses' arms was a Hollywood

118

tradition but Isabella had no grounds to complain. While her years in front of the harsh lights of a film set were written on her face, Isabella's figure would easily put much younger starlets to shame. Her ample breasts sat high on her chest and her arms, legs, and tummy were conditioned by years of rigorous calisthenics, yoga, and, more recently, jogging. For Isabella, the consumption of a few pastries was not going to be the start of a downward spiral to obesity.

Otilia removed a wine screw from her apron and proceeded to open the bottle with practiced skill. Isabella let the fingers of her right hand hover over the *Papanasi* as she considered which of the pastries would be best. The shimmer of her manicured, painted nails was not lost on Otilia, but she buried her jealousy deep.

"Oh miss!" said Otilia. "Look at you. Thin as an oak tree sapling, you are." Otilia popped the cork and rested the bottle between the two diners. She would often deliver praise to women and men alike if she thought a sizable tip would be left at the end of a meal or after a lengthy stay at the hotel.

Isabella was pleased with Otilia's words and took a bite of her selected pastry. The flaky crumbs of the Papanasi hung on her full, red lips as she spoke. "You're too kind. And, oh my god! This is delicious! Polina, you must try these."

Polina registered that the fragility of a well-prepared Romanian delicacy was enough for the memory of Isabella's agent's recent death to apparently become a thing of the past. She reflected how the ideals of communism stated America, and Hollywood in particular, were only vanity disguised as patriotic democracy. Polina was not a party member, and she did have thoughts that perhaps the situation in her country was not as ideal as the leaders would have her believe, but she did consider the narcissism of Americans to be a bit much at times.

The young waitress took her leave of the women and quietly closed the door as she exited the library. Unlike Crina, Otilia did not peer through the window after leaving. She had no interest in the investigation and especially with the nosy Russian guest taking charge when no one had asked her to.

Polina poured wine into the two glasses and handed one to Isabella before picking the other up for herself.

"What is it?" Isabella said. "Perhaps ten in the morning? The paparazzi would love this." She held the glass toward Polina in a gesture of friendship.

The women clinked their glasses together. Isabella breathed in the wine before taking a healthy sip while Polina waited without drinking any herself.

"I realize this may be difficult, but may I ask you a few questions?"

Another deep sip passed Isabella's lips. The relaxing effect was already showing. "Of course. I understand. I don't have anything to tell you, but I'll try." She rolled the stem of the glass between her fingers, which caused the wine to spin gently.

Polina returned her glass to the table and moved forward in her chair. She was aware what people did not say—what they held back either on purpose or by mistake—was often of greater value than the information they did share.

"Mr. Steel, was he a friend or a business associate?"

Isabella smiled and finished her glass of wine. She moved her empty wineglass in small circles while contemplating what to say. "Dan is—" Isabella said, but then corrected the error in her tense, "was, is more exact I suppose—my agent."

Polina was silently surprised by this choice of word. In her world, this label meant much more than perhaps how Isabella was applying the term.

"Agent?"

"I'm an actress, Dan was my talent agent. He was responsible for finding me decent scripts and great film projects. Recently, he had done neither." Isabella poured another glass of wine. She stopped only before the wine was about to spill over the rim of the glass. "Have you seen me in films?" Isabella already knew the answer and did not wait for Polina's reply. "Of course not. Not for a while, anyway." Picking up her glass, Isabella gulped a long and full mouthful. She set the glass down and dabbed at the corners of her mouth where a drop or two of the liquid rested. "I have Dan to thank for that."

"Last evening, he was in the hall with you. He appeared to be… how shall I put this? Well, more than your talent agent." Pointing out the obvious relationship between the two Americans would serve no purpose so Polina had chosen to be more obtuse.

"Oh that." Her face flushed with a consideration of regret as she wished she had avoided the whole sordid confrontation with Dan. "Yes, I suppose. Well, in the past, I suppose the feelings were mutual. I needed him for work, and he needed me for the money my employment brought him." The wine had barely had time to settle before Isabella placed the glass near her lips again. She hesitated and took another long sip before gazing out the window at the snow-covered trees. For a moment, Isabella longed to be somewhere else. "Yea, those lines blurred at times, but he was no more than an entertainment for me. Not what you would consider to be, how should I say this? Well, our non-professional relationship lacked an emotional bond. Let's leave it at that."

Polina had the appearance of a friend on her face, but inside she weighed each word and sentiment Isabella said with extreme care. As yet, Polina had no reason to believe Isabella was guilty of anything other than demanding sympathy and making poor choices in the bedroom. That said, Polina was well aware this woman was an actress and she, therefore, had the skills to play a character. One capable of hiding important facts in order to avoid suspicion.

"You know... my uh... my life," Isabella said, her voice and sentiment growing increasingly emotional. She bit her lip before offering a slight laugh of resignation. Her eyes were focused on the glass of wine.

"Every day, I live—" Isabella was choking up, but she pushed through. She breathed in and locked eyes with Polina. "I live every day in the unexpected. Every actress does. We all accept it as the nature of this horrid business. One day, you are an innocent, the next a rising star. Soon, your name is on the cover of magazines, and then... a nobody." Isabella finished her second glass of wine in one unladylike gulp.

Polina witnessed Isabella's eyes glazing over as tears crowded the corners.

"Perhaps a third?"

Polina took the glass from Isabella. Any more and Isabella would be useless to her. Isabella fell back into her chair.

"No. You're right. Too much, and too early." She resigned herself to being alone for the remainder of the trip and possibly not having any career to return home to.

Polina needed to get the questioning back on track before the actress passed out from the effects of drinking most of the bottle of wine before eating any breakfast other than a single pastry.

"What brings you to Romania?"

"Dan wanted me to meet with a producer here." Her tipsiness was showing. *I need to keep her on her toes*, thought Polina.

"Are you Romanian? No. No, you're Russian." Isabella waved a drunken finger in Polina's direction. "I can see that. Russian women are so beautiful. You are so beautiful." Isabella leaned toward Polina. Her finger now pointed away from Polina and toward her own face.

"Well, I guess the communist countries are not tired of Isabella Manson." She collapsed back into her chair with a look of resignation. "At least that was what Dan promised when he told me we must come here."

"And how long had Mr. Steel been your agent?"

"Twelve years. When I signed with him, I was young, popular, and beautiful. Now… not so much."

Polina needed more. The time had come to butter her up a bit.

"Oh, Isabella, please. You're gorgeous, and I'm sure plenty of important directors in the US and in Europe would jump at the chance to have you in their films. Perhaps you need a new agent?" Polina regretted her thoughtless question the moment the words left her red lips.

Isabella laughed out loud. "Well, I guess that option is now open!"

"Had Dan Steel always been a talent agent?"

Isabella shrugged. She clearly possessed little knowledge about the man or at least this was what she wanted her interrogator to believe.

"No. He had two jobs. Agent by day, and something else the rest of the time. I think he was also a lawyer or something for the government. I remember he said he traveled a lot for work. South America and Europe, mostly. Russia, too, I believe. You appear to know him. Did you ever meet him in Russia?"

Polina ignored the inquiry. She did, however, realize she had finally uncovered something familiar, something that might help her.

"One last question. Did you hear any loud noises during the night?"

Isabella lifted her purse from the floor and set the bag in her lap. She struggled to reach deep inside before finding what she needed. With an abundance of flair, she produced a pair of fur trimmed ear warmers. She pulled them down over her head and let them rest haphazardly on her ears.

"Elegant, aren't they?" she said. "I realize they're for outside, in the snow or whatever, but I can't sleep without them. So… sorry, nope, I heard nothing."

Polina pushed her untouched wine glass toward Isabella before standing and picking up her own purse.

"Here, you deserve this. Now, please excuse me as I need to find Crina and ask her a few questions." She regarded Isabella who has already started in on the glass of wine offered to her. *She is an odd one. That much is certain,* Polina thought.

"If I can be of any help, please find me."

"Thank you," Isabella said as she appraised Polina. She wobbled to a standing position and came close to her.

"Polina, will you find him? The killer? Do you think he is still here… in the hotel?" Her voice wavered as she spoke and her eyes began to water.

Polina reached out and grasped Isabella's free hand tightly. The gesture was one of kindness, as well as proving a stable platform for the actress to balance.

"You have my word." She held on for a moment longer before releasing Isabella's hand and walking to the door. As Polina stood in the opened doorway, she turned to face the American. Isabella was still standing where Polina had left her.

"Oh, one last question. Did you go to the swimming pool last night or perhaps early this morning?"

"No. Not my thing," said Isabella. "In fact, most would agree I can't swim. I prefer to keep an eye on the hunks from the comfort of a beach towel."

Polina smiled and left, closing the door behind her. She experienced a pang of guilt knowing Isabella was drinking herself into oblivion, but she had far more important things on her mind. Isabella would have to take care of herself, something Polina was sure she had been doing for more than a few years.

In the lobby, Crina was speaking with Everett Cook as his boyfriend, Christian, stood nearby, studying a tourist brochure he had pulled off a wooden shelf. Polina approached them. She had no plans to allow their discussion to get in the way of her investigation.

"Excuse me Crina," said Polina. "Where is the swimming pool?"

"Oh," said Everett, "sounds lovely." He turned to his travel companion. "Christian, my dear boy, what do you think? Should we have a bit of a swim after breakfast?"

Christian joined Everett at the front desk, his eyes on Polina.

"Will this fine lady be swimming... in her bikini?" Whether or not he was aware of the fact, his voice dripped with slime.

Everett was shaken. He appreciated Christian had a nasty habit of being a Horatian, but Everett had asked him to control his roving while he was picking up the tab.

"Oh, he does joke," said Everett. He spoke with an unsettling mixture of love and reprimand.

Crina paid no attention to the lovers. She understood Polina's task took precedent. She motioned with her hand like a stewardess as she explained.

"Halfway to the library, you'll see a door on the left. Through that, you will find a hall leading to our pool."

"Thanks. Oh, also, would you please put together a list of the guests? I will need to see their passports too."

Crina was uncomfortable such a request had been made in front of guests. She had hoped for more discretion from Polina.

"Um, yes… of course." She eyed Everett nervously as she agreed to the requisition.

"Thank you."

Before she turned to leave, Polina glanced momentarily at Christian but focused her attention on Everett. Something seemed familiar about the older man. Had she seen him somewhere before? In Moscow or perhaps in his native England? While she had no reason to suspect him of killing Dan Steel, she would need to track the British gentleman down and ask him a few questions, if for no other purpose than to answer her own nagging confusion on the matter.

Everett gave Polina time to walk down the hall before turning to address Crina.

"Is this about the American?"

Crina was shocked news of the death was already bouncing throughout the resort. Granted the hotel was a small, enclosed space, but she was still surprised the gossip had started so quickly. Almost no guests, she thought, and yet everyone is aware of exactly what is going on.

"Yes," she said as she controlled her anger at having to discuss the issue with Everett. "I'm afraid we had a small incident. Polina, I mean, Miss Tolkunova, is helping us look into what happened. Now if you—"

"Incident?" said Christian, who lacked the discretion and maturity of his gentleman friend. He leaned his bulky arms on the front desk and pulled in close to her. "You sound rather British, Crina. A man is killed in his locked room and you call that an… incident?"

At that moment, Crina wished for another corpse and hoped she would be held responsible.

"Please, we must let Miss Tolkunova do her job without too much speculation."

"Quite right," said Everett. "We must step aside but be ready to be as helpful as possible for the young investigator. Although I must say, I do object to having my passport handed over."

He tapped his walking stick firmly against the ground twice to make his point. "Bit of an incident in itself."

Chapter 7

The pool was once again still, appearing like a glacial tarn high in the mountains on a crisp spring morning. The room was empty as the guests were either sleeping or enjoying breakfast. Or in the case of Dan Steel, dead.

The giant doors swung open and Polina stepped into the room. She released the doors and they closed quickly behind her. The click of the lock resonated throughout the room. She was hit with an overpowering odor of chlorine; the same noxious tang she had encountered on Dan Steel's swimsuit and on his room's carpeting. The odor was not unpleasant, but it was indeed strong. She was sure no bacteria were hardy enough to survive under such harsh chemical conditions.

Polina moved further into the room before stopping to consider the sheer size of the space. She marveled at how perfect the public spaces of the hotel were: the lobby was immaculate and the library where she interviewed Isabella rivaled the best reading rooms in Moscow and others throughout Europe she had spent time in. And now this room: voluminous, yet personal and inviting at the same time. Razvan had done quite an amazing job bringing the old castle into the twentieth century. Polina wondered why the individual guest rooms were not as opulent. Perhaps Razvan had run short of funds when it came to decorating the bedrooms or perhaps, he simply lost interest.

Moving with no sense of urgency, she proceeded to the table stacked with precisely arranged blue towels. Eight stacks she counted. Seven of the neat piles had five towels each, but one pile was shorter with only a single towel. Was this recent? No, she thought perhaps the hotel staff had not replenished the towel Steel had taken back to his room the night before. But why were four missing and not only one? She picked up one of the towels and let it unfold as she held onto one corner. She brought the towel to her nose and breathed in its cleanliness. The luxury cloth was reassuring in both its perfume and absorbent texture. Without folding the towel, Polina dropped the heavy cotton cloth back on the table.

Like everyone who came to the room for the first time, Polina was drawn to the amazing wall of windows. She walked over to them and contemplated the gorgeous view outside; no one doubted the magnificence of

Romania's mountains. Snow covered every surface; from below the windows to the most distant hills. The only disruption in the continuous whiteness was a set of obvious tracks leading toward a battered work shed resting under a few small leafless trees. The drag marks in the snow indicated the building's doors had recently been opened. Polina presumed this was where Toma and Ilam had stored the corpse of Dan Steel.

As she turned away from the windows, Polina's left foot kicked an unseen bottle of vodka resting on the floor. The bottle tipped over and rolled along, stopping only when it hit the leg of a chaise lounge. A few remaining drops dribbled out and were quickly absorbed by the porous granite. On closer examination, the two shot glasses sitting on a nearby table jumped out at her. Like the bottle, one was on its side. She was angry with herself for not seeing the vodka and glasses earlier. Polina's job called on her to be aware of such tiny, seemingly insignificant details. *What's distracting me about this case?* she wondered. Polina bent at her knees and examined the glasses. The tipped-over shot glass showed nothing of interest, but the other, the one sitting erect on the table, had the distinct remains of dark ruby-red lipstick.

The sound of the sauna door opening behind her startled Polina. She stood and turned to see Anne-Marie emerge from the small room in a cloud of steam. Polina experienced an unhealthy attraction to Anne-Marie as she moved in what appeared to be slow motion. Her silk-like brown skin was jaw-dropping. She had seen other black women during her European assignments, but seeing someone of color in Russia was still a rarity. When she did come close to a black woman, their flawless skin always left Polina feeling somewhat less than perfect.

Anne-Marie was wearing a deep-red bikini sitting high on her hips. The matching top barely covered her ample breasts which moved in vigorous cadence as she walked. In one of her hands, she carried a blue towel and in the other a glass container of mineral water. She threw the towel into a basket on her way toward the doors.

"Excuse me." Polina's voice filled the air as if she had shouted in church.

Anne-Marie stopped still in her tracks and glanced to where Polina was standing. She said nothing. She simply stood and stared at her.

Polina walked at a pace indicating she was interested in having a significant conversation with the hotel's only guest of color. "Excuse me. I'm so sorry, may I ask you something?"

Anne-Marie stood her ground and waited for Polina to come near. "I guess. What do you want to ask?"

The two were face to face. That was not, in fact, entirely true. Polina was a woman of average height but her ever-present heels allowed her to measure up to many men and exceed most, if not all, women she came in contact with. Anne-Marie was the exception to this advantage. Barefoot, Anne-Marie still towered over Polina and her Afro hairstyle made her more imposing. Polina realized if she had worn flats today the difference in heights would have been farcical. Additionally, the contrast between Polina in her Italian heels, business blazer, and pencil skirt against Anne-Marie in nothing more than her skimpy bikini was striking.

"Are you a guest?" Polina said.

"Is that not obvious?"

Polina deciphered a wonderful blend of accents and dialects hidden under a cautiously pessimistic voice. She sensed polished French but also something from a Central or perhaps Northern African nation mixed into the spotless English delivery in this woman's voice. Polina realized Anne-Marie was not about to discuss the matter with this woman who had appeared out of nowhere. But she reluctantly continued.

"Yea. I'm a guest. What's the problem?"

"Oh no, no problem at all. I'm speaking with each of the guests. The hotel has asked me to look into an issue. I'm sorry, what is your name?"

"Anne-Marie. Anne-Marie Paris."

"What a beautiful name. Anne-Marie did you see—"

"The dead man? I presume you're investigating him... the dead guy."

Polina was taken aback that Anne-Marie was aware of the death. For a brief moment, she was unsure of how to proceed with her planned line of questions. Was Anne-Marie admitting to the assassination or perhaps she had seen something incriminating?

"Well, yes, a man died in one of the rooms last night. May I—" *No,* she thought. She needed to clarify the situation before moving ahead. "I'm sorry, did someone tell you about the death?"

Anne-Marie smiled. Her teeth were as white as her skin was black and also perfect. Jealousy, or perhaps something else, something not entirely foreign to Polina, rippled through her body, but she wouldn't allow Anne-Marie to see her exposure.

"No need," she said. "I saw the two men."

Polina's eyes brightened. A lead, perhaps? But two men... Not the scenario she had imagined when examining Steel's room.

"You witnessed someone leaving Dan Steel's room? When was that?"

Anne-Marie enjoyed having the upper-hand. She was also aware the woman asking the questions was more attractive than the average white woman and this pleased her.

"No, I didn't say that. What I said was, I saw the two men." Anne-Marie pointed to the wall covered in windows where Polina had previously been standing. "Two guys, they were taking the body to some shed or something. It was actually rather comical."

"I'm sorry, can you explain?"

Anne-Marie had no interest in a lengthy conversation with Polina. That was not the reason she had come to the Teleki. As a black woman, she had become accustomed to white men and women asking questions and doubting the answers she gave. She did not consider any of them racists, although she had battled with more than a few of those over the years. Instead, she always believed for some reason she needed to justify who she was and what she was doing. Blacks were finally making progress in civil rights and Anne-Marie had linked arms in many protests to advance the cause. Inside, she was twitching and hoped a quick explanation would satisfy Polina's questioning.

"All right, well, it was earlier this morning. I was sitting over by the big windows." She pointed to the window wall before walking to the table covered in fresh towels. Grabbing one, Anne-Marie dried the perspiration from her chest before continuing her story. "I heard some noise. People talking, arguing really. The noise was coming from outside, so I got up to see what the racket was all about."

"Can you show me where?"

Not excited about spending her morning discussing the matter, Anne-Marie hesitated before walking with Polina to the window. She pointed to an area to the right of the flat terrace, the hillside dropped steeply toward a group of tall trees twenty meters lower. Something had disturbed the snow on the slope as the surface was not as smooth and continuous as it was on every other part of the hill.

"These two guys, no clue who they were, they were struggling with a big, bulky tarp or something. The one guy, I figured he was like, from Morocco or some other country in North Africa, he's bitchin' and moaning about not wanting to help. I remember now. He said he was a chef. Perhaps the resort's chef, I don't know. I don't really care. Anyway, he's going on and on and the other guy, handsome and tall, he was telling him to shut up and suddenly, the chef guy trips and falls."

"Had you seen these men before? Here at the hotel, perhaps?"

"No. Like I said, one was a chef and the other guy was like a maintenance worker or something. Anyway, the maintenance guy, he's in charge I think, he starts screaming at the chef. Saying stuff like 'Oh come on! Lift, damn it.' The other guy is sitting on his ass and yelling back, saying he's a chef, not an undertaker or some shit like that. The chef stands up again, and they're plugging through the snow like Laurel and Hardy."

"I'm sorry, who?"

"The funny guys, you remember, from Hollywood. Old stuff I guess, but still groovy."

Polina gave her a look of understanding although she was still unconvinced. She was intrigued by Anne-Marie's vernacular. The words were familiar, but they still sounded strange as she had not encountered anyone in person who spoke this way. She only heard this language style on news reports about civil unrest in America.

"Anyway, the maintenance guy asks, 'Why did Crina tell us to do this?' I don't know who that is, do you?"

"Yes, she is the hotel manager. You probably met her when you checked in."

"Oh yea, cool chick. Front desk, right? Well, this guy is going on about why should he have an idea of what to do with a dead body and why does this Crina chick think it's his job. Right about then, a bunch of snow crashes down from the roof and about buries these two idiots. They fall and drop the tarp they're carrying and it goes tumbling down the hill. The tarp hits a rock or something and bumps into the air and starts unwrapping and this guy's body comes flying out and splats into a tree. I thought I was watching the whole thing in slow-motion. Sorta cool, really."

"The body is loose and hits a tree?" Polina was not sure whether to laugh or remain resolute. Either way, she had to admit Anne-Marie told a fascinating tale.

"Yea! That big one"—Anne-Marie pointed to a sizable tree with less snow than any of the others— "down that hill. Kinda weird, actually. He was like a children's floppy puppet, arms and legs bouncing all over."

"So, you saw all this happen?"

"I was laughing. Good thing those guys didn't hear me, I guess. I mean, come on, this show was like seeing a really bitchin' comedy on the telly. The chef starts yellin' about how he wanted to leave the dead guy in the tree, saying he's gonna be cold enough and he would be as frozen stuck to the tree as he would be in the tool shed. The other guy was having none of it, calling the cook a lazy shit and saying he was amazed they allowed him to boil an egg. He shoots back that all the maintenance guy does around here is screw some bird named Otilia or something. It was so cool to hear guys talking when a chick isn't around to distract them. You know what I mean, right?"

This was indeed something Polina sympathized with. She had listened to more than a few conversations coming from behind closed doors between male contemporaries, and she found them all childish and rather disgusting.

Satisfied she had related the story, Anne-Marie turned to face Polina.

"You see, quite a shitshow. Two idiots and a dead body. Made for Hollywood, man, made for Hol-ly-wood!" She said her last words with power and pulled upon more of an African nation dialect to bring the tale to a natural close.

Polina had to agree. The story Anne-Marie had related sounded entertaining, if not macabre.

"Please, if I may, are you here alone?"

"Exactly how I prefer my life. Me and my God. I don't need anything or anyone else."

Polina glanced at the vodka bottle and the shot glasses. Only then did she realize Anne-Marie's lip color matched the lipstick on the glass. Rather than call her on the potential lie about being here alone, Polina took a different path.

"What room are you staying in?"

"I'm downstairs. 117. Why?"

"And you were in your room last night? Did you hear anything unusual? During the night or early morning hours?"

Anne-Marie's patience was wearing thin and with the line of questioning now turning more and more personal, she was looking for a way out of everything Polina was posing.

"I thought you only had a question or two. This is becoming a bit of an interrogation." She took steps to skirt around Polina. "Yea... I heard nothin' last night."

Polina did not attempt to stop her. She let her walk past and found herself looking briefly at Anne-Marie's tight bottom and admiring her amazing tone. *Not a drip of cellulite on her,* Polina thought. She reeled in desires she had never before acknowledged and dashed over to join Anne-Marie as she walked toward the exit. Polina made a mental note to do an extra set of squats each morning from now on.

"Are you are from France? I sense a French accent."

"French Polynesia originally, but I live in England now."

Polina had never had an opportunity to visit the islands of the South Pacific. Bali and Tahiti were on her bucket list, but so far, she had not received an assignment that would fulfill such a dream.

"What do you do? In England, what is your job?"

"I'm a phlebotomist." She stopped but kept looking forward.

Polina perceived the tension in her forehead and the woman's breathing indicated she was about to explode.

"Look, honey, I'm going to my room now to shower and unless you plan to join me..." She winked at

Polina. "Well, I do hope you find the killer. I'm sorry I couldn't be of more help."

Anne-Marie quickened her pace, increasing her distance from Polina while decreasing the number of steps needed to leave the room.

Polina took several long strides and caught up with her near the door. She positioned herself between Anne-Marie and the door.

"I'm sorry, what's a phlebotomist? I'm not sure I'm familiar with the job."

In reality, Polina was quite aware of what Anne-Marie did for a living, but she needed her attention for another minute or two.

Anne-Marie was not about to let this tiny Russian woman block her exit. She reached past Polina, making no excuse for bumping her out of the way, and pulled one of the doors open. Anne-Marie stood in the doorway, her foot holding the door, and faced Polina. The light bouncing of the still waters of the pool put Anne-Marie in the sort of glow all women longed for. Somehow, she appeared more beautiful as the few remaining drops of perspiration glistened on her taut belly. The warm air of the sauna had accentuated her perfume and Polina found the aroma intoxicating and wanted to ask what brand she was wearing.

"I draw blood. You know, I put needles into people's arms and take blood samples.

"One last question, I promise. Why are you here? What brings you to this area, this hotel?"

"I'm on my way to Bucharest. I'm teaching a seminar on a new technique for taking muscle biopsies." Anne-Marie held up a finger on both hands, indicating a distance of about twenty centimeters. "Bit bigger needles. Rather nasty, but fun." With a devilish smile and matching laugh, Anne-Marie let the door close behind her.

Polina's mind was spinning. A long needle would have been an appropriate weapon to kill Dan Steel, especially if the person using the needle was skilled in how and where to push the probe in. This also accounted for a lack of blood at the crime. She finally had a suspect, but an important aspect was missing, something every crime and criminal needed.

A motive.

Simon King

Chapter 8

Crina was leaving the front desk with a handful of passports and a single piece of paper as Polina returned to the lobby after questioning Anne-Marie.

"Ah, Miss Tolkunova—I mean Polina. I was coming to see you. I have the list you asked for."

"Perfect. Thank you."

Polina took the list and scanned the names. Without looking up, she motioned for the passports Crina was holding. "May I?"

"Yes, of course," Crina said as she hesitantly handed the documents to Polina. "Here, but I think it best if you leave them with me after you've examined them. I am sure some guests wouldn't appreciate knowing I gave their personal documents to another guest. This is actually quite inappropriate. I'm sure you understand." Whether she did or not, Crina had no plans to allow Polina to walk off with the valuable documents.

Polina took the passports. She had no interest in retaining them; she only needed to put names and faces together along with the country of their primary residence. Beyond that, she had no reason or desire to keep them in her possession.

"Of course, yes, I understand. I will look at them quickly and return them right away."

Polina stepped to the front desk and opened the first passport. By coincidence, and perhaps most appropriately, the document was Dan Steel's. His residence was listed as Los Angeles, California. The passport was almost expired with less than ninety days left until the document would be useless. Flipping through the passport, Polina was struck by the empty pages. Isabella had mentioned he had traveled extensively while working for the American government as a lawyer, but his passport showed no indication of him being in any country other than England and Romania. She thought perhaps his international travel had been on a previous document. That would explain the barren status of this one.

Placing Steel's passport on the desk, she moved to Isabella's; she found nothing out of the ordinary in hers. The passports for Christian, Alejandro, and Lilla were also unremarkable. Márta's document, however, contained a few surprises. This was a woman who had traveled to almost every country in Europe multiple times but had stayed in each one no more than a day or two. She also had a five-year visa for travel to Russia and the stamps in the passport indicated she had made abundant use of such permission. Polina opened the last passport as Crina spoke.

"Oh, by the way, Mr. Cook wishes to see you in the dining room."

Polina considered this piece of information with puzzlement as she was presently examining his passport. She held the passport open to the identity page and showed the photo to Crina.

"This man?"

"Yes. Everett Cook. He's waiting in our restaurant. He asked me to send you in when you were finished at the pool."

Polina flipped through the pages of Everett's passport. *Well-traveled,* she thought, *but other than that, nothing out of the ordinary.* She gathered the passports into a small stack and handed them back to Crina. Polina smiled enthusiastically.

"Well then, we must not disappoint him, must we?"

Crina accepted the passports and anxiously held them between her hands before placing them in a drawer behind the front desk and locking the drawer securely.

"Are you making any progress? Do you know what happened to Mr. Steel? Do you know why someone would want him dead?"

"Too early yet. Some pieces of the puzzle are coming together, but much remains to be learned and uncovered. Some facts I don't know, but I'll discover those, given time." As was Polina's style, this was not entirely true, but she knew of no reason for Crina to be informed.

Polina wrapped her hand around Crina's in an effort to calm the young lady. She held her hand for a moment before indicating the door to the dining room.

"In there, you say?"

The comforting motion noticeably relaxed Crina. After the past few hours, she had now reached a point where she believed in Polina's confidence and her uncanny ability to handle the situation without any apparent stress. She admired her and considered if she was capable of doing the sort of work Polina was busy with. Polina's actual occupation still eluded Crina. This detail nagged at her as she wondered if the Russian woman was perhaps no more than an amateur sleuth playing out a mystery-novel fantasy at the expense of Mister Steel and the hotel. But as this idea crossed her mind, she was unable to think of any reason to believe such a thought to be true. Polina was honest and had not irritated any of the guests so she had no reason to stop her queries at this point.

Polina entered the restaurant, which was empty of all guests except for an older gentleman sitting alone at the table nearest the window. The morning light gave the room a warmth, making the death of a guest seem inconsequential. As Polina walked across the room toward Everett, she saw his table was carefully arranged with a stainless-steel rack of toast, an open-top boiled egg sitting in a tiny pink cup, and full tea service all resting on a crisp white tablecloth. A small crystal vase with a sprig of fern and a single nondescript flower was centered on the table.

Everett himself, many would say, was overdressed for the occasion. He wore a tweed three-piece suit and tartan tie. Although hidden under the table, his black shoes were polished to a blinding shine. Everett was reading yesterday's copy of *Le Figaro* as Polina approached unnoticed.

She stood at the table for a moment, taking him in before introducing herself.

"Excuse me, Mister Cook? I am Polina Tolkunova, I understand you wish to speak with me."

Everett peered over the top of his paper at the enchanting lady standing before him. His eyes brightened as he realized the woman was Polina. He folded and placed his newspaper on the table, straightening it imperceptibly before addressing Polina.

"Ah! Excellent. Here you are." He stood and pulled out the chair next to him for Polina. "You look quite beautiful on this rather challenging morning. Please," he said, indicating the seat.

Polina accepted his graciousness and sat as he pushed the chair gently closer to the table. "Such a gentleman."

He took his seat and gazed at Polina in a way that made her comfortable. His eyes had a warmth and his

147

weathered face made him into an ideal grandfather who was interested in everything one might wish to tell him, no matter how mundane. Everett Cook would accept you regardless of your flaws and without reservation.

"Now, what will you have, my dear?"

Polina realized she hadn't eaten anything yet today. Her investigation had occupied her every moment from when she first left her room. Was now the time to relax? She decided she would wait a while longer. This meeting was backward and for now, she needed to understand why Everett had asked to speak with her rather than she requesting to sit with him.

"Oh nothing, I'm fine. Thank you, though. But please, don't let me interrupt your breakfast."

"Nonsense! One cannot track down a killer on an empty stomach."

Exactly like a grandfather, Polina thought as she remembered how her mother's father had always been so kind and attentive. After the murder-suicide of her parents, Polina had been sent to Sevastopol by the Black Sea to live with her maternal grandparents. She was still a schoolgirl at the time, and the next ten years would be formative in who she was today. Every morning, she awoke to a cup of hot chai seasoned with heaping spoonfuls of sugar sitting next to her bed. Her grandmother would prepare a breakfast of toast and oatmeal, and later Polina would walk with her grandfather through Park Pobedy to the coast where they would swim in the warm waters of Sevastopol Bay.

After WWII, the Presidium of Supreme Council of the Russian SFSR issued an order, labeling Sevastopol a closed city as the location was the southern port for the Russian fleet. On visits to the city center, Polina would stare as countless men in military uniforms hurried from one building to another. When she asked her grandfather what these men were doing, he would always change the conversation by offering to buy her sweets or ice cream. These days would be filled with laughter and wonderful tasty meals of borscht and pelmeni. On weekends, they would take a small bus to her grandparent's tiny dacha in the mountains overlooking Yalta on the Black Sea. Polina remembers nothing but happiness during the years she spent with them.

Everett motioned to Otilia, who was busy setting a table nearby. Without finishing what she was doing, Otilia set down the silverware and came to Everett's table.

"Yes, Mister Cook?"

"Now, what will breakfast be Miss Tolkunova? What can this fine young lady bring you?"

Everett's sentiments produced a smile from Otilia. Once in a while, she encountered a guest she enjoyed and Everett Cook had been an example of that rare event. Realizing she was fighting a losing battle, Polina gave in and turned to Otilia.

"May I have some tea, please?"

"Of course, ma'am."

Food was important to Everett, and he was not going to let her get away with such a minimal request.

"No, no, no. That will not do." Everett eyed Polina, taking her in. His eyes were warm and non-threatening. She was taken aback as her heart beat noticeably faster as she imagined meeting a man like him, but forty years younger. "My guest will have yogurt, a mixture of fresh mountain berries with clotted cream, and a small bowl of muesli with whole milk. And, of course, tea with milk and sugar." Everett smiled and winked at his breakfast companion. He was satisfied with his ability to read Polina. This faculty was among the many skills he had acquired over a lengthy career. "Yes, perfect. Thank you, Otilia."

Polina was impressed. Most men would either ignore her needs or would have suggested a more masculine breakfast of bacon, eggs, and potatoes. She had, in fact, always preferred to eat a light meal in the mornings.

"Well now, you are quite amazing. I would think you almost know me." She returned his smile. "You certainly know what I enjoy for breakfast."

"I'm not performing magic, my dear. Look at you, thin, attractive but strong, glowing skin with the minimal use of cosmetics and not a blemish to be seen anywhere. And your hair, healthy and flowing like a young child's." He stopped to let his comments soak in, but not long enough for a response. "Clearly you avoid the British fare of boiled ham and overcooked eggs with a dash of yesterday's tinned beans. No, you are far too refined for all that tosh."

Polina attempted to hide the blush growing on her face, but the pink flush would have been evident to everyone in the room if it had not been empty. "You are too kind, sir. Thank you, Mr. Cook."

"Everett. Please. I was never completely satisfied with that surname, but we work with what we are given. Isn't that right... Polina?"

First her surname, then her choice of breakfast, and now the familiarity of her first name. She recalled he had been standing nearby when she requested the passports from Crina. Had he found an opportunity to look through her own? While Everett apparently had a vast knowledge about her, Polina realized she understood almost nothing about this odd gentleman sitting across the table from her. One thing she was sure of: the time had come for her to focus the meeting and lead the discussion. She decided a matter-of-fact approach was needed if she was to stay one step ahead of this sly old fox.

"The receptionist said you wish to speak with me. How may I help?" She straightened the placement of silverware before her, letting him realize she, too, had the ability be precise and inquisitive.

"Yes, quite right," Everett said as he sipped his tea without taking his eyes off Polina. "Crina is wonderful, isn't she?" He placed the teacup back into its saucer and rotated the combined china no more than two-degrees until the cup's handle was parallel to the table's edge. "I understand she gave you the information you needed. Names and passports and all. I trust the details made for interesting reading. Knowing as much as possible about those you are investigating is of utmost importance."

Polina realized he had succeeded in turning the conversation, once again, to be about her.

"This Dan Steel fellow, bit of a bother I would say. What have you gleaned about the chap?" Everett removed a slice of toast from its metal rack and, using a small knife, placed a dab of bright yellow butter precisely centered on the bread. He spread the butter confidently and methodically in a circular motion making sure the toast was covered from edge to edge. He was talking his time preparing his next words, for he was sure they would surprise Polina. "I met him, you know. Had a few, shall we say… tête-à-têtes with Mister Dan Steel over the years." He nibbled the corner off the toast and chewed slowly as he waited for her response.

This news hit Polina like a bolt of lightning. At the same time, she was satisfied this meeting might be more useful than the previous two interrogations. *Perhaps another step toward solving the crime,* she thought. Regardless, she believed remaining stoic rather than satisfying Everett's own inquisitive nature was in her best interest.

"You were acquainted with Mr. Steel?" Polina said in a calculated voice. "What sort of meetings? Are you an actor too? I understand he was Miss Manson's talent agent." Polina examined Everett with care as he jiggled in his seat. She wondered if perhaps he was enjoying her questions a bit too much, rather than finding them troublesome. She caught a sinister smile growing on his face.

Everett dipped his buttered toast deep into the cracked egg and took a small bite of the soaked bread before setting the remainder on his plate. Picking up a napkin, he wiped his lips and held the cloth motionless in his hand as he contemplated his next move. Having chosen his forthcoming words with care, Everett sat the napkin down meticulously and moved forward, ever so slightly, in his chair.

"Do you know who I am? And please, we have no secrets here. I am too old and too"—he paused to make sure the next word would sink in properly—"experienced to waste time on trivialities and subterfuge." A new group of wrinkles appeared as he narrowed his eyes.

Polina was lost. She was sure control of the conversation had shifted dramatically and this did not please her. For the first time in her investigation, she was not in charge.

"I'm sorry. I looked at your passport, but the document only indicated retired."

Everett sat back in his chair. He placed his right hand on the sculpted top of his walking stick, massaging the shiny structure with his elderly fingers. Polina was not sure what the carving on the stick's head was, but perhaps it was the head of an animal. *A fox,* she decided although the beast might as easily have been a bear or perhaps a fish for that matter. She wondered if the sculpted figurehead carried some meaning for the old man or if the cane had been the most expensive one the London atelier had offered for sale.

"Retired. An interesting label. Is that why I carry this bloody walking stick? Do we ever retire? I mean, from this business. What we do is in our blood. Retirement is not in the cards. We either die of natural causes or we are killed; retirement is never an option."

"I'm sorry, Everett, I am afraid you have me at a loss." She realized this was a weak response, but she needed more time and more information before she could properly engage this man. In addition, he was leaving her in a sad state of confusion. Something she did not appreciate.

Everett removed his hand from his walking stick and picked up his teacup. He took a lengthy sip while never taking his eyes off Polina.

She was sure this pleasant grandfather guise was an ingenious cover for the devilish character laying deep within.

He moved the cup of steaming liquid to his mouth and took a long drink. As he did this, Otilia arrived with Polina's breakfast, which she arranged before her on the table.

"Ah! Precise timing. Polina, you are Russian, of course, so I am sure you appreciate the essence of precision and the necessity of exactness."

Again, this Brit was proving to be too smart. Not only did this infuriate Polina, but his knowledge also made her all the more anxious to learn more about him than his passport had shown. She was surprised to see him playing such an intricate game; one she had played many times before herself. But this was vastly different. Everett was a master, and he was painting Polina as a novice.

Otilia poured a cup of tea for Polina and set the teapot down near her plate.

"Anything else, ma'am? Mister Cook?"

Polina smiled, but before she could answer, Everett took over. Once again, setting the meter as to how everything happening at this meeting would progress and who would be responsible for moving the tête-a-tête forward.

"This is wonderful. Thank you so much, Otilia. I am sure Miss Tolkunova will enjoy this fine meal. Please pass along our gratitude to Ilam."

"I will, Mister Cook, thank you." Otilia returned to her duties setting other tables. She enjoyed serving Mister Cook for not only was he kind and gentle, but he also tipped remarkably well for an Englishman. Previously, she had discovered the British were exceedingly tight with their spare coins but Everett had never failed to reward her nicely. This was not the first time he had visited the hotel, but usually he came in the summer months and stayed a full week. In the past, he had traveled alone and his tips had doubled her weekly salary but this trip, perhaps because of the presence of his lover, his gratuities had been much grander.

Everett indicated the various bowls of yogurt, muesli, and berries arranged in front of Polina. "Now, please, Polina, have some breakfast. I do hate to eat alone and to have such a gorgeous and professionally-dressed guest joining me, makes this much more of a shame. By the way, have you met Ilam? He is the chef here. A remarkable young man with amazing talents with a saucepan." He leaned forward and lowered his voice. "Quite the ladies' man, I would imagine. Handsome looks and all."

Polina picked up a small spoon and retrieved a single raspberry, which she dipped into the yogurt. She had decided slow and steady was the best, and perhaps the only course of action when dealing with Everett Cook. At least for now. She slipped the food past her red lips and let the mixture sit on her tongue. The tartness of the yogurt complimented the sweetness of the berry. She had to give Everett credit; he was an expert in choosing a meal. She swallowed almost imperceptibly and spooned another berry—a blueberry this time—and as before, dipped the dark blue ball of fruit into the yogurt. Polina let the delicious food linger there before leaving the spoon to rest in the bowl like an abandoned flag on a battleground.

"As you said earlier, I am rather busy this morning. So, let me ask you some questions. To start, you said 'Dan Steel's killer.' Why do you think he was killed?"

Excellent, Everett thought. She was finally moving ahead with the right line of inquiry. He decided he would give her the rope she needed to hang herself.

"While you have the advantage of having examined the body and the room, I assure you his murder is as obvious to me as the assassination is to you."

"If you will excuse me, that makes no sense. How can the reason for his death be obvious, Everett, if you lack the facts?" She picked up the pace. "You also said you had previous meetings with Dan Steel. How? Was he an associate or a friend?"

"You disappoint, my dear Polina."

If Everett was attempting to lead Polina down a path of his choosing, she was not interested. "How is that?"

Everett began to feel overwhelming frustration with the young woman. He had expected so much more from his Russian contemporary. He found himself unnecessarily arranging his silverware as he contemplated how to push the young investigator in the correct direction and help Polina with her duties. Technically speaking, helping Polina was not his responsibility at all. In fact, there would be many at the Home Office who would frown upon the relationship and chastise him severely. But after countless years globe-trotting from one assignment to the next, Everett had reached a point where he wished to help the other side in hopes of creating a more satisfying world culture. Returning his attention to Polina, he took a deep breath and exhaled slowly.

"Dan Steel was an agent. But of that, you are already aware."

"Yes, he was Isabella Manson's talent agent. He—"

Despite his best efforts, the conversation had become too much. Everett grasped his walking stick and pounded the cane aggressively against the floor. The impact echoed from the kitchen to the lobby. For the first time, Polina was rattled. She had not expected this rash action from the dignified Mister Cook.

"Stop!" he said. At the edge of losing his temper, Everett collected himself. He took his hand off his walking stick and straightened his coat and tie before looking into Polina's eyes. "I will be clear—crystal clear—so we may speak as equals." No, this was not the word he was looking for since Polina's few years in the field were no match for his decades of experience. "Well, contemporaries perhaps."

What followed was an ominous lengthy pause while Everett watched for any change in Polina's facial expression. There was none, which he took as a positive sign.

"I am sure you are aware, for your handlers will have told you, Dan Steel was an agent—a spy if you prefer—working for the CIA in America." Everett let his words sink in for a moment. He could almost hear the gears grinding to a halt in her head as she shifted mental direction. "His cover was, and has been for years, as a talent agent. This was an effective ruse, for it allowed him direct access to a certain breed of American citizens considered to be communist sympathizers. The movement in the states had been growing since its formation in 1919. This, of course, is after the Great War but also, and of more interest to your country, after the October Revolution. Once the messy business with Hitler had come to its fitting end, the Communist Party of the United States of America, as it was now called, began picking up pace. Over the ensuing years, Hollywood evolved into the headquarters and breeding ground for this far-left political movement."

Polina, of course, was aware of all this information, but she was not prepared for Everett Cook to be schooling her in this manner. For perhaps the first time in her career, Polina was unsure if she should let down her guard or instead, object to Everett's declarations. For the moment at least, she decided to remain silent and sat perfectly still, staring at him without saying a word.

"But, as I said, you already have this information… Comrade Tolkunova." He threw the title in there with enough sarcasm and assurance to make Polina bristle. Within seconds, her lips tightened as she pulled her head backward.

"You see, you are right in being bothered, for I know quite a bit about you, Tovarisch Tolkunova."

Everett rotated his hand back and forth on the head of his walking stick to let his words sink in. If she had been uncertain about the breadth of his knowledge about her, she was about to find out.

"Where shall I begin? Top of your class from the Russian police academy in Moscow with an emphasis on the forensics of violent crime scenes. Soon after, the KGB came knocking. Dead parents, no siblings, no love interests… strange that, actually. There must have been many men who wished to share their desires with you. I am sure you had more than one night in a dismal hotel far from the relative glamour and comfort of Moscow feeling lonesome and looking for someone to help you relax and forget the task you had been assigned."

Everett let a planned smile escape to allow her a bit of breathing room before he continued. He was proud at how he had played her to this point, but he was also impressed she had held back from delivering a heated rebuttal.

"Regardless, you were a clean slate with nothing to muddy the waters, so the KGB shipped you off to Tatarstan where you learned your tradecraft. First, as a honey trap, which was never to your liking and I do not blame you. Such an ugly business. All too often men can be terribly basic. But now, look at you, a full-fledged *Shpion*, a spy. A much more dignified occupation for a woman of your stature and intelligence, I'm sure."

Now Polina took a long sip from her tea while keeping a watchful eye on Everett. Polina realized the cat was far removed from the bag at this point. *What is his end game?* she thought.

"Your presence here," Everett continued, "at this beautiful hotel among these amazing mountains during a raging blizzard, is no more remarkable than my own. You came here during a dark Romanian winter to"—he spoke slowly now with an emphasis on every word— "meet your contact. Who was, of course, our departed friend, Mister Dan Steel."

Everett dipped a new slice of brown toast in his egg but did not eat any of the combination. Instead, he let the warm bread hang from his fingers as the yolk dripped onto his plate. Polina realized this was the first, and perhaps the only time, he allowed something sloppy to happen in his presence.

"But someone removed him from the equation before you could meet up. Rather sad, actually. Dan had been a decent man. Dedicated to God and country and all, I mean outside of the whole spreading-Communism-across-America nastiness. But as a spy… well, clearly, not his strength." Everett took a sizable bite of the toast slice, which he chewed slowly and swallowed. "Apparently, Dan Steel grew tired of working for only one country when he could as easily pull in two paychecks."

"And you?" Polina said. "MI6?" She already had deduced this was the case, but hearing the answer in his own words would be beneficial.

"There was a time. But now, as the passport indicates, retired."

This was now a chess game and Polina looked to make only the right moves going forward. She had not played poorly up to this point, but he had proved himself a tactical master. With each uttered word, he had manipulated her and placed her exactly where she was needed. Polina had no way of knowing Everett had a reputation for non-lethal techniques to get the most out of a captured enemy and had been called on numerous times to deliver lectures on the subject to incoming British agents.

"Let's say, for the moment, I accept your various claims. But, the question remains, why are you here?"

Everett winked at seeing Polina taking charge and a slight smile emerged. He was aware from her background she had the ability. He had only needed to tickle the skills out of the young agent.

"Ah! Excellent catch. All right then, perhaps not fully retired." He placed his hand on the stick, tapping the cane lightly against the hardwood floor. "But, as this blasted appendage indicates, not quite operating at full strength anymore."

Polina stared at Everett intensely. She was not about to let him play the weak-and-frail-old-man card. Everett's cane was by his side, not to help with walking, but rather something to lean on to drive his points home. She was no longer going to excuse him for his age; she had come to that realization. Polina needed to treat the Englishman as the adversary he had proven himself to be.

"I am sure you will appreciate the British government is in the same raft with our allies, the Yanks. We are both equally interested in communist infiltration among our citizens. I was tasked with meeting Dan once he spoke with his contact. That being, of course, you. I planned to do a bit of catching up. I'm sure you understand."

"And yet you believed he was acting as a double agent?"

"Precisely. We were aware, as were the Americans. Both agencies were monitoring him carefully. Have been for some time now."

Polina was ready to place Everett in check. Not quite checkmate, but close enough to cause some anxiety. *Why not put this old spy on the spot?* she thought.

"Perhaps you killed Mr. Steel. I would say you had a motive." She tilted her head and let her lips remain open a fraction after she spoke.

"As a double agent Dan Steel was an asset. However, he was sloppy, so we were able to feed him information that he delivered to your side, and we were aware of exactly what to think about the response he returned to us. This was reason enough to keep him in the field. The British and the Americans had no interest in eliminating Steel. Far from it, actually. His death comes at a poor time for us, but we'll come out on top. We always do."

Everett placed his silverware on his plate, arranging the knife and fork just so. He poured a small dash of milk into his teacup. As was his style, every movement, every action was dedicated and precise.

"I understand. Today, you and I are enemies. At least that is what our governments want us to believe. But the truth is never so simple. Am I right, tovarish? I am well aware you have had to eliminate people who you didn't necessarily consider to be an issue. But you obeyed orders. I've done the same over many years. This is what we must sometimes do."

Everett raised the teapot and poured the pleasant-smelling liquid into his cup. He followed this action with two compact sugar cubes and stirred the mixture quietly before continuing.

"At the same time, I am sure you have had occasions to go against protocol and process someone despite the order to leave them alone. I believe there was an incident in Warsaw last year."

Polina did have a rather unpleasant encounter in Warsaw the previous January. Her local Polish contact had become too familiar and was blackmailing her. In exchange for keeping her cover clear, the man had demanded sex. And not simply a night of rolling around together; he had required perverted domination of her. At one point in the evening, she had stood naked in front of the man and asked him to completely undress. His disgusting sneer had exposed several gold teeth, and he proceeded to do as she requested. As he pulled off his pants, Polina had reached into her purse and put an end to the arrangement with two bullets in his heart and one dead-center in his oversized, sweat-dripping forehead. Moscow had been furious, but as her record had been otherwise remarkable and once her handler understood the threat posed by the man unmasking her, she was allowed to remain in the field. Polina was under the impression the entire incident had been kept at the highest levels of secrecy within Moscow, but Everett's acknowledgment of the assassination made her understand her handlers had been sloppy with their promise.

Polina removed the spoon of yogurt and berry and placed the mixture on her tongue. She held the empty utensil vertically as if to punctuate her words. "And now what, you want me to... trust you?"

"Would this be too much to ask? Well, I suppose the best way for you to decide if you should trust me is to"—Everett sipped his tea and set the cup down— "trust me."

As Polina considered the ultimatum, she was unaware eyes were watching the two of them from across the room. In the kitchen, Ilam worked at the oversized central table preparing food for the lunch menu. With a substantial knife, he chopped vegetables on a cutting board and scooped them into a bowl.

A collection of cooking utensils, including a long, slender meat thermometer, lay scattered across the table. Otilia stood nearby, looking through one of the doors, which she held partially open. Through the gap, she was able to spy on Everett and Polina at their table.

"Why is he talking with her? She comes here in the middle of a storm and now she has the run of the hotel. I mean, who the hell is she?" Otilia's fingernails scratched across the surface of the stainless-steel door.

"Has she asked to speak with you?" Ilam said. "I guess she's asking questions about the dead guy. Did you know your lover made me help him move the damn body?"

"Toma," she said as she let the door swing closed and turned toward Ilam, "is not my boyfriend." She was not a girl who would allow herself to be tied to a single relationship. Yes, she had slept with Toma, but Ilam had also received the benefits of her attention. On occasion, she was not below sleeping with a hotel guest if he happened to meet her criteria.

Otilia took up a position on the side of the prep table opposite Ilam. She was a different person in the kitchen than she was with guests. Her salty Ukrainian roots emerged and she never held back. If Razvan or Crina had seen her acting as she was now, there was no doubt she would be reprimanded or, more than likely, fired.

"Toma is something to occupy my evenings. I need something to relieve the stress of this damn job. You know this, so don't try to play innocent."

"How do you think he feels about you?"

"I don't give a shit. We screw. Nothing more. I feel nothing for him and I sure as hell hope he feels the same. Probably not though, I mean he is a guy. You guys are always so clingy and needy. Why can't having some fun in bed be enough? Screw and move on."

Otilia picked up the meat thermometer and balanced the sharp end on the tip of her finger. She instinctively understood exactly where the utensil's center of balance was for the thermometer stood at attention on her slender appendage.

"So, are you going to speak with her?" Ilam said.

"Do you think I would answer to her? She is no one to me. Sometimes, the guests here are so full of themselves with their money, their furs, and their attitudes. She's no exception. She may have Crina bowing down to her and giving her everything she needs, but as for me…" Otilia flicked her finger and the meat thermometer launched into a high spiral flight before landing, point down, digging into the table. "She's no more than another Russian slut."

Ilam finished chopping the carrots and celery and set the knife down on the table. He gathered the vegetables into the oversized stainless-steel bowl and moved to a nearby sink. As he washed the vegetables a second time, he continued to address Otilia.

"Crina said she wants to speak with everyone. This woman—I think her name is Tolkunova—she says that Dan Steel guy was murdered in his locked room. What makes you think she's Russian?"

"Yea, that's her name, Polina Tolkunova. Oh, and yes, she's Russian. But why do I care where she's from?"

Otilia picked up the knife, moving the blade from hand to hand with no thought needed. For a waitress, she had tremendous skills with sharp instruments. She had learned them as a teenager when she worked with her parents in a traveling circus. Otilia was the young girl who was strapped to a spinning circular target while a man threw knives at her, barely missing her arms and legs. That man had taught her many knife tricks, which she had not forgotten after so many years. She had also not forgotten he was the man who took her innocence behind a trailer one night. The experience had been horrific for her and when her father found out two days later, he beat the knifeman to a bloody pulp. That had been Otilia's last day working in the circus.

"Let her come to me. Let her ask her questions. We shall see what she learns."

Otilia spun the knife in the air, caught the blade by its handle as the shimmering steel flew past her face, and drove the knife into the table with a resounding firmness. The knife wobbled back and forth as she removed her hand. In a final act of defiance, she knocked over the meat thermometer, watching the utensil roll across the table and come to rest against the knife's shining blade.

Chapter 9

In the parking lot, the air was still and the landscape straight out of a snow globe. The aroma of winter was intimate and the falling white was now a small percentage of what dropped from the skies the day before. A short distance from the entrance to the hotel, the silhouettes of two women, both wearing long fur coats, stood silent.

Márta fidgeted nervously with an unlit cigarette as Lilla kicked at the snow. While this gathering would have been a reasonable one for them to be enjoying the fresh air and scenery after being trapped inside by the storm, that was not the case. The tension between the two was obvious.

"You worry too much," said Lilla. "You know that, right?" She took a step forward to where a clump of snow invited her foot. In a mighty swing, she scattered the pile into the air. The flakes hung for a minute, glistening in the late morning sun, before falling to the ground like so much white on white. If Lilla had made the dramatic move to make a point, the effectiveness of the action was now lost. "My life is not for you to be concerned about. What I do with my free time is for me to think about, not you. You know, not everything I do needs to concern you. Come on, Márta, I'm an adult, I'm a woman. You remember being young and with a man, don't you?" Her final words made Lilla's skin crawl as she imagined the woman in bed with her father. This was not something that took much imagination, for Lilla had soon discovered when Márta moved in she was not what one would consider to be a quiet lover. In fact, demanding might have been a better term.

Márta called this meeting as she was not pleased with her stepdaughter. From their first days together, the relationship between stepmother and stepdaughter had been contentious. This had been especially true whenever Lilla's father would leave town and the two women were trapped under a single roof.

"Wrong!" Márta's voice raised an octave as the word spit forth. "This is my job. It is my responsibility to worry about everything when it comes to you!"

Lilla shook her head in anger and disgust. She was having none of this.

"Says who? Not my dad. That's for sure. He may well have decided to let you into his life, but that does not mean you can force yourself into mine. And it certainly does not make you an equal to him in my opinion." Lilla strutted to where Márta stood and grabbed the cigarette from her. She placed the unlit tobacco between her own lips. Lilla had never been a smoker and found the habit disgusting, but this action against Márta made her feel dominant. "You should have selected a different partner for this little trip of yours." She yanked the cigarette from her mouth to drive her next point home. "A nun, perhaps."

Márta grabbed the cigarette from Lilla and wiped away any evidence of the girl's deep red lipstick. She removed a shiny metal lighter from her pocket and clicked it once and then again before a flame formed. Márta placed the cigarette in her mouth and held the glowing lighter close to it, but did not light the cigarette.

"Lilla, it's simple." The cigarette bobbed up and down in her mouth as she spoke. "All I ask is you keep a low profile until we have an opportunity to leave. After that, you may screw anyone… and everyone, for all I care. But while we are here, as mother and daughter, keep your skirt on and your knees together."

"You're so disgusting." Lilla narrowed her eyes and she shook her head as she spoke. She spun on her toes in the snow and turned to go back to the hotel only to come face to face with Polina. The surprise encounter made Lilla take a full step back.

"Oh my! You startled me."

Polina was wearing her mink coat over her suit and skirt. Her hands were covered by the gloves she had worn the night before during her drive to the hotel.

"I'm so sorry. I did not mean to make you jump."

Márta turned quickly and faced Polina. She had anticipated there would come a time they would meet. She was aware this woman was asking questions of all the guests.

"Good afternoon, ladies. I was told I might find you out here. Crina said you had come out to enjoy the sun finally making an appearance." She looked up at the sun's rays breaking through the scattered clouds. "Beautiful, isn't it?" Fresh from her revealing discussion with Everett, Polina needed to make some progress in her investigation, and Márta's passport chocked with visas and stamps of passage made her the ideal next guest to interview.

Márta nervously buried the lighter and cigarette deep into her coat pocket. Within a second or two, her face became calm and welcoming.

"Why, hello," said Márta. "We were just heading in, actually. It is beautiful, but still bitter out here. At least the wind has died down a bit." She took an exaggerated deep breath. "There is nothing quite like the mountain air in Romania."

"You were looking for us?" asked Lilla. "Why?"

"Lilla, please. I am so sorry. You must excuse the young girl. Politeness is a skill she lacks at times. I'm afraid that is a trait of many girls of her generation." Márta was being careful not to place Polina in the same age bracket as Lilla, but in her mind, anyone under forty was ignorant and ill-informed.

"No, it's fine." Polina thought back on her meeting with Everett and reminded herself not to let the Hungarian trick her with pleasantries and small talk. "You might be aware there was a death in the hotel last night."

A look of devilish interest sprang to Lilla, and she moved closer to Polina.

"Someone died? Who? Was he murdered? Who did it?"

Polina shifted her attention to Lilla. Rude, perhaps, but talkative, which was always useful during an interrogation.

"I didn't mention murder. I simply said someone died. Why would you think it was a murder? And why do you think it was a man who died?"

Lilla wasn't concerned by Polina's direct questions. She was accustomed to speaking out and defending herself. She was never worried if the other person was in a position of authority or not.

"If someone died naturally, there would be no need for you to ask questions, would there? So, I presume this person must have been killed. It's always a man, isn't it? I mean, a woman might be more interesting, I suppose. So, the dead person's a man, right?" Lilla enjoyed a well-orchestrated bit of back and forth and was able to hold her own against anyone. She had acquired the skill from her father. 'Negotiation is like a tennis match,' he had told her. Her father insisted she return every question with several of her own, which must hit harder and faster to keep your opponent off-guard.

"Lilla, please don't be so gruesome," said Márta.

"Who are you, anyway?" said Lilla. "Are you the police?"

"My name is Polina Tolkunova. You are Lilla Karády, is that correct?" Polina eyed Márta. "And her... mother, I believe. Márta. Is this right?"

Márta stepped between Polina and her stepdaughter, jumping at the opportunity to avoid Lilla answering and perhaps making things more complicated than need be.

"Yes, that's right. How can we help? I assure you we know nothing about this man and his murder." Realizing she had chosen the wrong word, Márta corrected herself. "I'm sorry, his death. Dying at a beautiful hotel like this one is so unfortunate."

The woman's decision, like Lilla's, to label the deceased as a man was interesting to Polina, as she had carefully left the fact out yet both of them jumped to the same conclusion.

"Perhaps we can go inside," said Polina. "Much more comfortable in there."

"Of course. The warmth of the hotel sounds most appropriate at this moment. Shall we?" Márta indicated the hotel's entrance with her extended arm.

Polina led the way to the resort's front door as Márta shifted her head back to witness Lilla dragging her feet.

"Come on, my dear. I am sure this won't take long."

Lilla sneered her disapproval of having to spend even one more moment with her stepmother, but at least there would be some excitement over the discussion of a dead man in the same hotel she was staying at. She would have some juicy gossip to share with her friends back home.

Polina unbuttoned her mink coat as she crossed the lobby to where Crina was speaking with Toma. She was unable to hear them, but their animated expressions told her this was not a friendly conversation.

"You never said this was part of the job. I refuse!" said Toma. His temper was only a few degrees below a full boil.

"You can't! When I came here, I made it clear. Do you remember? And Razvan—your boss, in case you forgot—also explained this to you. I was there when he told you."

Crina was in a heated state too, something Polina had not thought possible.

"Cleaning up after a murder was not part of the deal. That much I do remember. And now, you are demanding I do this? Why am I always your errand dog?"

Crina became aware of Polina approaching and didn't want her hearing their argument. There was no reason to involve Polina, as the disagreement had nothing to do with her or the investigation she was leading. "We will continue this discussion later. In private," she said.

Toma stormed away toward the kitchen. As he passed the three women, there was no pleasant smile or polite greeting. The anger in his eyes said everything.

Crina made herself busy, quickly adopting a happy face as Polina reached the counter.

"Ah! You found them. Wonderful." She moved around to the front of the desk and stood next to Polina. Unlike the towering difference between Polina and Anne-Marie, imagining these two women as sisters, both in height and appearance, was not difficult.

"Yes. Thank you. Rather cold out there, so we will move our discussion to the library."

"Oh, I do believe Mister Serrat is in there at the moment. Perhaps I can find another—"

This announcement excited Lilla and she pointed down the hallway.

"Down there, correct?"

Not waiting for an answer, Lilla took off down the hall. Her enthusiastic approach did not register well with Márta, but she said nothing. She would continue reprimanding her promiscuous stepdaughter later.

"Mr. Serrat," said Polina. "He's the gentleman from Spain. Am I right?" She was aware of the answer to her question, but there was no reason to show off her memorization skills to the other women.

"Yes. He's a writer, I believe."

Polina took this in and faced Márta. This was not a detail included in his passport as his occupation had been listed as a professor at the University of Barcelona.

"Well, if you don't mind, Miss Karády, perhaps we can all speak together. It would speed things along a bit."

Márta was unable to decide if she liked the idea or not. On the one hand, she would have the opportunity to confront the Spaniard, but perhaps that face-to-face meeting would be better without the Russian woman present. Put on the spot, she chose to allow Polina to have her way.

"Of course. That is fine with me. If this Mister Serrat does not mind, it's fine."

Lilla and Alejandro embraced in front of the library's fireplace, which burned with a passion equal to their own. No one would mistake the extent of their relationship, if not be a bit taken aback by the dramatic and obvious age difference. Lilla had removed her long coat to put her curves on display for her lover. Alejandro wrapped his arms around Lilla's slender body. With one hand, he cupped her tight butt cheek while the other pulled her close so her firm breasts pushed hard into his own sturdy chest.

"You're so cold, my dear. Why on earth were you outside?"

"Márta is all bent out of shape about something and wanted to scold me. She is so"—Lilla paused to find the best words to describe her stepmother— "ancient and prudish. I'm sure she has never experienced the pleasure of a man. At least not a man like you." She quickly washed the image of her father in bed with Márta from her brain.

Lilla pulled Alejandro closer, feeling his love growing against her. He had not been her first lover, but he had proven to be her best. She had developed early and by her first year of high school, she resembled a woman in all her form. This led to increased attention from the young lads in her class, as well as upperclassmen. Lilla found herself pulled toward the older boys, the ones who had grown facial hair and would be sent to mandatory service in the army twelve months later; these were the men that attracted her the most.

Her first sexual partner was a slim, athletic lad named Grisha. She had turned sixteen only a few days prior, and he was barely eighteen himself. They made love only once and the event had been clumsy and brief, impressions which made her wonder why women bothered. But then Kolya came into her life. He was older than Grisha, and far more experienced in lovemaking. A math and science genius who would go on to study nuclear physics in university, Grisha made Lilla laugh and had a set of moves that pleased her in bed. This was the relationship that convinced Lilla an older man was what she wanted and needed to be a complete woman. Her father and mother had both approved of him, which made everything so much easier. When he left for university, she had cried for weeks, believing she would now be forever lonely. But for Lilla, this was not to be the case.

"What did Márta want to talk to you about?" He had no interest in her answer, but Alejandro wanted her to believe he was concerned.

"Oh… I don't know. Who cares? Anyway, we were about to come back in and that Russian woman was standing there. She appeared out of nowhere. Right in my face. Scared the shit out of me."

"The Russian woman who's asking all the questions?"

"Yea, that's her. Polina something, I don't know. They're coming here now, Márta and the Russian. I think she wants—"

Alejandro's demeanor changed dramatically, and he pushed himself away from Lilla. She stood there, feeling alone and confused. Men had never wanted to leave her embrace before.

"Polina Tolkunova? She's on her way here? Why? What does she want?"

Lilla was none too pleased with Alejandro's sudden and unnecessary distancing. *Does he realize what he has here?* she thought.

"I don't know. I mean, I guess she's asking questions about the man who died in his room last night. She is like a policewoman or something. Some guy was murdered and she's investigating. So what? Anyway, why are you being so weird suddenly?"

"Is that what she told you? She's asking about the dead man What did you tell her? What did Márta say?"

The library doors swung open and Polina and Márta entered. Seeing this, Alejandro stepped even further away from Lilla, an act which increased the anger boiling under the surface of her olive skin. He moved to a nearby table where his leather satchel was unlatched with the bag's contents spilling out. Among the items on display were a glass syringe with a lengthy needle and a bottle of liquid medicine. Alejandro shoved the syringe into a small metal case and pushed this into his satchel. He straightened his papers before placing those in the bag too. He believed he had done this quick enough to avoid any attention being drawn toward his belongings, but Polina had a keen eye and had effectively inventoried each of the items, including the needle.

Márta came close to Lilla and wrapped her arm around the young woman. She held her tight, despite Lilla's squirming attempts to gain her freedom. As Márta hugged her stepdaughter, she kept her eyes focused on Alejandro with equal measures of suspicion and disgust. Lilla gave up on trying to break free and attempted to smile, but her discomfort at being in Márta's arms was a distant second to the anger she held toward Alejandro.

"You found us!" said Lilla. "Oh no, now whatever will we do?"

Márta remained unimpressed by Lilla's attitude. There was going to be hell to pay when she got the girl alone and again when they returned home to her father.

"Yes, and apparently..." Márta cast an evil eye on Alejandro. This was a woman who would not back away from going toe-to-toe against the most controlling of men and bring them crying to their knees. "Just in time."

"I'm sorry. What are you implying?" said Alejandro. He realized how Lilla's stepmother was acting and her voice left little doubt things were about to get ugly.

Despite her earlier decision, Márta didn't hold back. "You should be sorry, you pig. Do you know how old she is? And what? How old are you? Old enough to be her father? Can you not find women your own age? Why must you hunt down little girls?"

"Listen, lady, I don't know what you think you know, but I do not need to sit here and listen to your baseless accusations."

This back and forth was of little interest and even less use to Polina. If they continued to bicker, interviewing the three guests was going to be completely useless. She stepped forward to address Alejandro.

"Mr. Serrat. Am I correct? My name is Polina Tolkunova. The hotel has asked me to speak with the guests in hopes of gaining some understanding about a—"

"She wants to know who killed the dead guy! You didn't do it, Alejandro, did you?" said Lilla.

Alejandro was smart enough not to be distracted by the young woman, especially as he was sure Márta was one step away from physically attacking him. Instead, he pushed his hair back and examined Polina, hoping to alter the course of the meeting.

"Well," he said, "I can assure you it was not me. Why would I be involved?"

"Oh, no. I am not here to accuse, I am trying to find out if anyone can help me understand what may have happened. You know, ask if someone heard anything or perhaps witnessed anything out of the ordinary." Polina watched at Lilla and Márta standing at the fireplace, appearing less like stepmother and stepdaughter and more like two people who had never met before. "And of course, why this gentleman was killed in his room."

"Are you with the police?" Alejandro said.

"I already asked her. She won't say." She may have been the youngest person in the room, but this minor point was not about to hold her back from participating.

"It's not that I won't say, I am—"

"So, you're not a doctor and not a policewoman," said Alejandro. "And yet, you're interrogating the guests? This seems a bit odd, to say the least." He realized his attitude was defensive, but he didn't care. He had reason to be concerned.

"Interrogate is a strong word. I was more hoping you and the ladies could help me. I am only asking questions. You are, of course, not compelled to answer." Polina realized she needed to break the stalemate lingering in the room. She motioned to the. immense oak table which sat under the ornate chandelier hanging over them like God witnessing their attempts at the truth. "Please, perhaps we could all sit?"

Polina and the others found seats around the table. Alejandro took care to position himself closest to the door and Lilla pushed her own chair close to him. The seating arrangement was one Alejandro wished he could change, but to do so now would draw unwanted attention. Márta sat opposite Lilla, but her focus remained on Alejandro. The scorn she held in her eyes toward the Spaniard could melt diamonds.

"What would you like to know?" said Márta. "I'm willing to help in any way I can, but I'm not sure how."

Polina smiled inside. Márta was playing the typical move of getting out in front of an investigation in hopes of drawing attention away from her. She decided to let Márta believe her technique was working.

"You and Lilla are here together, is this correct?"

Lilla sat back in her chair and crossed her arms. The grumpy young woman had returned to her true form.

"Not my choice." She glared at Márta before switching her displeasure to Polina.

Márta reached across the table and offered Lilla a kind hand, which she did not take. Rather than be angry, Márta withdrew her peace offering and smiled at her instead.

"Yes. We arrived a few hours before you. We came by taxi from town. We arrived before the storm started to cause problems. I'm amazed you were still able to drive on that road! That highway is so steep and windy."

Without unfolding her arms, Lilla moved forward in her chair while continuing to stare at Polina. In return, Polina paid no attention to her.

"And why are you here? Why did you come to this wonderful hotel in the middle of winter? Was this a planned holiday for you and Lilla?"

"I would imagine we came here for the same reason as you; a weekend away."

"Bit of a long trip from Hungary, though. Is it not?"

Márta glanced at Lilla with something approximating love. "We needed some mother-daughter time together. I had been here before, several years ago and I remembered how relaxing the resort was."

Polina turned her attention to Alejandro. But before she could ask him anything, he jumped in.

"To write. I came here for some peace and quiet so I could finish a book. And now this. Questioning from someone I don't know about something I know nothing about. I find all of this unpleasant. Tell me, why is a Russian citizen with no legal authority in this country asking questions of me, a Spaniard, about a murder of an American in Romania?"

"I understand. Please, humor me for a moment." She was doing her best to be pleasant to the man, but he was not making that easy. "You are a long way from Spain. Barcelona, I believe. Why would you leave the warmth of the Costa del Sol to come to Romania in winter?"

"Costa Brava. The Costa del Sol is along the southern coast near Marbella. Closer to Gibraltar."

Polina knew this, but wanted to test his reaction. "My apologies, Mr. Serrat."

"Anyway, as I said, I came here to write. The warm waters and bikini-clad women offer too many distractions to a writer. Besides, the fresh mountain air inspires me."

The mention of other women ran up Lilla's back like a venomous snake. Locking her hands under her chair, she moved away from Alejandro as if having a childish tantrum.

"What room are you in?"

"One fifteen."

"And were you in your room in the early morning hours last night?"

"Of course. I was writing."

"You write in the middle of the night?"

Alejandro was becoming less and less amused by the situation. He squirmed in his chair hoping the fiasco would soon be over. "Must I repeat everything? It is peaceful then, in the middle of the night. There is nothing and no one to distract me. You are obviously not a creative person. You would not understand." Alejandro realized he needed to say more to get this woman off his back. "However, I do remember hearing a loud sound or something from the second-floor last night. At 3:30 in the morning, as I recall."

Lilla hesitantly peered at Alejandro. While she enjoyed his attention to detail in the bedroom or the sauna for that matter, she was developing a general uneasiness when she thought too much about him. Her narrowed eyes were not lost on Márta. Nor Polina.

"You are quite specific. Are you are sure of the time, Mr. Serrat?"

"Oh, absolutely. I checked the time when I heard the sound. I was surprised to hear something so loud at such an hour. It was impossible to imagine anyone else was awake in the hotel to make a noise. To be honest, the interruption prompted me to get some sleep before the restaurant opened for breakfast, so I went to bed immediately following."

Something was bothering Polina. Something did not quite add up. She glanced at Alejandro's wrist and realized he was indeed wearing a timepiece.

"May I see your watch, please?"

He was visibly shaken by the request He pulled his sleeve back enough to show her the gold adornment on his right arm. This was not the timepiece of a poor writer or college professor.

"No, I'm sorry, could you take it off for a moment? I promise to treat it with care."

Agitated but unwilling to create a scene, Alejandro unbuckled the wristwatch and handed it to Polina. She examined the jewelry carefully for a moment and returned it to him. As he was strapping the watch back on, Polina turned to the grandfather clock behind her and then turned back to Alejandro.

"Your watch is not set for local time. How did you realize it was 3:30 when you heard the sound?"

Alejandro pulled his sleeve down over his watch and brushed back his wild hair. It did not escape Polina that he was a handsome man and imagined he would have no problem securing the attention of any number of women. She also understood he was biding his time so he could plan his response.

"It's not so difficult to account for the time difference. My own city, Barcelona, is only one hour ahead. I am only here for a few days, so I have no need to adjust my watch. I do the needed calculations in my head."

Polina listened to his answer but decided against mentioning the time change was actually in the other direction. Was he ignorant or perhaps flustered? Instead of pointing out his mistake, she turned her attention back to Márta and Lilla.

"May I ask, are you sharing a room?"

Lilla laughed at the concept.

"I'm not a child," Lilla said. "Uh, I need my privacy."

Polina smiled knowingly. She had read Lilla perfectly right from the start. Polina was sure Lilla would not be pleased to learn she considered her no more than a typical teenage girl struggling with her identity. She was young, and that was her fault.

"Of course, I understand. What rooms are you in?"

"Lilla is in 113," said Márta, "and I am down the hall from her in 110. But I didn't hear anything last night. I am afraid I had a headache, so I took a sleeping pill." Márta surveyed Lilla. "Lilla, honey, did you hear anything?"

"Yea, maybe." She glanced at Alejandro. "I was"—Lilla thought for a second— "no, I guess not. I was asleep. I didn't hear anything."

The room fell quiet. The only sounds were the crackle of the fireplace and the ticking of the grandfather clock. Alejandro fidgeted in his seat. He sensed an opportunity and decided to break the silence.

"Is that it? Any other questions for us or may we continue with our lives?"

Polina was lost in thought for a moment before she snapped back to the present. She realized she would only have this one chance to get answers from the group, and she did not want to release any of them too early.

"No, I think we are done. Thank you. I think I have bothered each of you enough."

Alejandro was the first to push back in his chair. The sooner he could be away from the angry eyes of Márta and the insinuating inquiries of Polina the better. The whole room and the occupants irritated him to no end. Lilla stood also, she had questions for Alejandro and needed to be alone with him to get answers. She had expected so much more from the man she thought loved her. At that moment, Polina raised a hand indicating she was not quite done.

"Bear with me, I'm sorry. Had any of you met Mr. Steel before?"

Alejandro and Márta shook their heads. A little too fast for Polina's liking. Typically, the innocent need to think about a question like this so they can recall their movements and convince themselves of what they would say but the Spaniard and the Hungarian were unusually prepared. Lilla was another matter.

"I remember him. He was in the restaurant last night, getting drunk with some lady. They were arguing about something. Remember, Márta? The waitress wanted to give us a table near them but you wanted to sit next to the window."

"Yes, Lilla is right. I do remember seeing him when we went to eat."

The tone in her voice was not convincing. Perhaps this was an innocent enough recollection, but Polina still found it odd Márta claimed to have forgotten ever seeing Dan Steel when first asked. "Oh, him," said Alejandro. "Yea, he was sitting next to me. He and some lady, I guess she is an actress from Hollywood. Anyway, they were having an argument about her not getting enough acting jobs. But I had no idea who he was. I certainly didn't realize he was the guy who got murdered." Alejandro was even less convincing.

Polina was troubled Alejandro all of a sudden remembered so much about a man when only moments before he claimed to have never seen him. Alejandro had said all he had to say on the matter, and he waited no longer before grabbing his satchel from the table and heading to the door.

Lilla had hoped he would wait for her. But he did not, which she mentally added to her growing list of frustrations she had with Alejandro. *Is he like all the others?* she thought.

"Hey, Alejan—" She corrected herself to avoid angering Márta any further. "Uh, Mr. Serrat, wait, I wanted to ask you something."

The door closed and Alejandro was gone. Lilla took steps to follow him, but Polina stepped in front of her. For a woman who was no taller than Lilla, she could sure be effective in halting forward movement.

"I'm sorry, one more question, if I may."

Lilla did not appreciate this interception of her plan to catch up with her lover. She did nothing to hide her contempt for the situation or for Polina.

"What! Why do you have so many questions?" She flipped her hair back and scowled.

"It's a bit delicate, but if you will allow me."

"Of course. Anything to keep young Lilla away from that old man."

Lilla was about to explode on Márta, Polina, Alejandro, or anyone at this point.

"It seems Lilla has a different accent than you and fails to have any resemblance—"

Lilla jumped at the opportunity to distance herself from Márta.

"I'm from Ukraine. She's Hungarian. So?"

"Lilla is my husband's daughter from a previous relationship."

"I see. And why didn't he join you? Your husband? Why isn't he on holiday with the two of you?"

Lilla glared at Márta, her words sarcastic and biting. "Yea... Mom." She put a heavy emphasis on her last word. "Why isn't Daddy here?"

Márta was ready for this line of questioning. She had been for months. In fact, Márta was always prepared to defend herself and her husband. Perhaps this was the result of living under a regime where secret police and nosy neighbors routinely asked probing questions.

"My husband's job requires him to travel internationally. He is in England at the moment." She punctuated her response with a pleasant smile.

"I see. Well, again, thank you for your time. You have both been most helpful."

Lilla was already marching toward the door in hopes of tracking down Alejandro. Polina considered the mistruth she had said to Márta and Lilla. Yes, this had been a lie, thanking them for their help in the investigation, but she had an obligation to maintain a facade of friendliness with the women. For now, anyway, but that may not be the case later on.

Simon King

Chapter 10

So much had happened since Polina encountered Isabella and Crina in the hallway that morning. Now, as she climbed the stairs to her room, she needed to consider all the information she had gathered up to this point and clear her mind of dead ends so she could better appraise the potential leads.

Halfway up the squeaking stairs, her thoughts were interrupted by Christian Caine descending at an abnormally quick gait. He fumbled with a small silver object but, upon seeing Polina, he pushed whatever he had in his hands deep into his trouser pocket as he came to a crashing halt.

"Good morning," he said. His words came across as forced and only intended to politely satisfy Polina before moving on. He purposely avoided extended eye contact with her before continuing downward at a more conventional pace.

Under any other situation, Polina would have returned the pleasantry and otherwise ignored the guest. She would simply have gone about her business. But today was not an ordinary day.

"Excuse me, Christian, correct?" she said. She was quite aware who he was, but she also understood the question would necessitate a response and one that would require him to stop and face her.

Christian came to an immediate halt. "Uh, yes. That's right." Despite his best efforts, the awkwardness of his response could not be ignored.

"I'm sorry isn't your room on the first floor?"

"Yes... yea. My room is downstairs. I should probably, uh—"

"So why are you up here? Are you lost?" She was not about to let him get away with such a trivial answer.

Christian hesitated. He turned his gaze toward the lobby, looking for a release from the present situation. He began motioning with his hands that perhaps he needed to be elsewhere.

Polina had witnessed this action many times before; when people are caught in a lie, they start gesticulating aimlessly.

"I just thought I would see what was up here. Just exploring the Teleki... searching for secret rooms." After uttering the last few words, Christian seemed to grimace. Polina could sense he expressed regret for the choice of phrasing.

"And? Did you find anything interesting? Anything... secret?"

"No. No, afraid not, actually. Rather dull up here." He gave her his best runway smile, hoping that would be sufficient and stepped down one step. "I, uh, I need to find Everett. He gets a bit lonely if I am gone too long." Another step downward.

"If I may, how did the two of you meet?"

Christian's demeanor switched like electricity surging into an unlit lamp.

"Why do you ask? We're friends. Nothing more to say."

The line of questioning was not leading her anywhere. She needed to change tactics while she still had him as a captive audience.

"As you are aware, I'm investigating the murder of Dan Steel. His room was upstairs." Polina motioned with her hand. "Right up there. Second door... on the right."

"Yes, I did hear he was killed up there. Pretty gruesome stuff... not what you expect to encounter while on holiday."

"Where were you at about three in the morning?"

"Sleeping, of course. I am a heavy sleeper so I heard nothing. Probably slept right through whatever commotion there may have been"

Why did he offer this last piece of information? Polina thought. *I hadn't asked if he heard anything.*

"Was that a knife you had in your hand a moment ago?"

Christian's eyes darted from side to side as he considered how to answer the question and how he could excuse himself from the meeting entirely. He reached into his pocket and retrieved a silver folding knife. "Yes, this was my father's."

He held the knife out for Polina and she accepted the folded blade as he continued to speak.

"He left this knife for me in his will. I believe they call it a soldier's knife. Everyone in the Swiss Army carries one."

Polina examined the multi-bladed tool. The silver casing had a distinctive Swiss flag logo on one side. In addition to a folding knife blade, there was a flat blade screwdriver and a slender pointed awl. Although the plastic case showed little sign of wear, the awl and blade both had numerous scratches on their surfaces.

"Your father was Swiss?" She handed the knife back to Christian.

"Yes. I was born there, too. He died shortly after I was born. My mother and I emigrated to the UK a few years ago." He caressed the knife in his closed palm.

Polina sensed remorse and a longing in his voice, something she had not expected from the young man.

"Well, I have kept you long enough. Enjoy your exploring." Polina smiled and started back up the steps.

"And you too. Good luck with finding out what happened to that guy." With that, Christian turned and descended to the lobby taking the steps two at a time.

Like every other person Polina interviewed, Christian had no obvious reason to murder Dan Steel, but he also seemed vague and not completely forthcoming with facts about his life and other details surrounding the crime. She considered this rather strange unwillingness to be honest and open as she approached her room. What were they hiding and why? In the past, Polina had found when people are interviewed about a crime, they would divulge more information than asked for in hopes of being helpful and, possibly, to cover up their own guilt.

Polina reached into her purse to retrieve her room key when suddenly a shiver of concern rushed up her spine. This was an impulse she had developed over many years. Like a sixth sense, she would become aware of a problem before the situation manifested itself. She carefully considered her surroundings and came to the conclusion there was no obvious reason to be concerned. Perhaps she was not fully recovered from her restless sleep the night before.

Sliding the key into the lock, she pushed the door open. Immediately, she realized her premonition had been correct. As she stepped into the room, Polina understood something was not quite right. A scent she could not identify lingered in the air. The odor of men's cologne or perhaps a woman's perfume, mixed with body perspiration. She had not whiffed any cologne on

Christian, but she wasn't particularly close to him when they met on the stairs. Regardless, this was not a pleasant smell and the pungency burned her nostrils.

Without advancing further, Polina reached into her purse and pulled out her gun. She never wished to use her sidearm, but she always understood the possibility existed. When she had used her weapon in the past, the action was always carefully planned and each shot had been precise and effective. This situation was different. She had to be ready to react with split-second muscle training and accuracy. Polina held the gun in front of her with two hands. This was the technique she had been trained to use in all situations where there was the potential of unknown assailants.

The bathroom door was closed, so she stepped past the room to where the bed was. The bed cover was no longer tight and smooth as she had left it in the morning. Her concern was now validated, and she tightened the grip on her weapon. A quick scan of the room revealed nothing else troublesome. She moved to the far side of the bed to confirm no one was hiding there. She was prepared for anyone and anything. Satisfied the bedroom held no immediate dangers, Polina moved back to the bathroom door. Reaching a hand forward while staying protected behind a wall, she pushed the door open. No sound came from the small room, so she whipped her body into the doorway with arms flexed and trigger-finger ready. The room was also empty and an examination of the counter and shower told her no one had entered the space.

Lifting the back of her jacket, Polina pushed her pistol into her skirt. This was not the most comfortable position, and the steel suppressor rubbed painfully against her buttocks, but she was trained not to place her gun on a table or somewhere else that would not allow her to grab the pistol rapidly. She was insulted and a little frightened to think someone had broken into her room. There was perhaps nothing more irritating than knowing someone had invaded her personal space, regardless of how temporary her time at the hotel might be. Many questions ricocheted in her head. Who had entered her room and how? Did they have a key or did they pick the lock? But most importantly, why had they broken into her room and what were they searching for?

Polina opened her suitcase and realized its contents were not as neatly arranged as she had left them in the morning. Each item had been lifted and set aside to allow someone to dig deeper into the case. Even the small cotton bag she had placed yesterday's underwear in had been examined. She always folded her panties with care before putting them in the bag, but they had since been removed and shoved back in with no attention to their previous arrangement. *What did they think they would find in my dirty undies?* she thought. She never kept any important documents or files in her suitcase. Before each assignment, she memorized the necessary background paperwork and considered every detail of related photographs and maps. Her passport and personal belongings were always stored securely in her purse. She was certain whatever someone had wanted to find in her room, their search had been fruitless.

Arranging the contents of the suitcase back to their previous carefully packed condition, Polina locked the valise and turned her attention to the rest of the room. There were no other belongings of her own to consider, but she had hoped to find some trace as to who had been there. A few minutes of hunting for those clues led to no conclusive evidence, and she decided the room was clean. Perhaps the invasion had simply been an intrusive maid searching for money or something of value to sell on the black market.

Polina went to the bathroom and used the toilet. She relieved herself while cradling her gun in both hands. Polina pondered the past assignments which had brought her to this particular hotel at this time. Everett had intimate knowledge of her life and career she believed were locked away in secret files. She always operated as if no one on the assignment knew anything about her. Polina would arrive at the location of engagement, do what had to be done, and leave before anyone would wonder why she was there and what she was doing. The meeting with the British MI6 agent in the restaurant an hour earlier had rattled her. Had she been sloppy on previous jobs? When did she come to the attention of the British Secret Service?

She placed the gun on the counter and pulled up her underwear and tights before flushing the toilet and washing and drying her hands. A casual glance in the mirror to check her hair and makeup was followed by moving to the bedroom where she retrieved a tiny bottle of perfume from her purse and dabbed a drop behind her ears and between her breasts. She returned the perfume and her gun to her bag and headed into the hallway.

Pulling the door to her room closed, Polina placed the key near the lock but stopped before inserting the key fully. Around the keyhole were a series of scratches she was convinced had not been there when she first entered the room the previous night. They were also not there when she left the room in the morning. She had a keen eye for details and her memory was never called into question.

She walked across the hall to Isabella's room and examined the lock on her door. The brass fitting was polished and spotless with not a single scratch. She turned again and went to Dan's room. Her heart rate increased noticeably when she perceived an almost identical series of scratches on the lock of his door. She was now convinced whoever had broken into Dan Steel's room and murdered him was the same person who had entered her room. She was also sure whoever entered the rooms had not been a hotel employee as they would have a passkey. No, these marks were made with some tool or device, not a key. This was not the work of an employee; this had been done by one of the guests at the Teleki.

Polina decided the situation at the hotel was becoming more dire and personal. She pulled her gun from her bag and once again secured the pistol in her waistband, this time under her jacket for more rapid access. Satisfied she was prepared for whatever may present itself, she headed to the stairs.

Polina crossed the lobby toward the restaurant where she saw Lilla waiting. Crina was working at the front desk and they exchanged smiles as Polina passed. For a hotel with so few guests, Polina wondered how Crina kept herself busy. In the summer months, she was sure the resort would be abuzz with dozens of visitors all demanding attention, but now there were less than ten.

The doors to the restaurant were unlocked but a small sign positioned atop a polished metal pole indicated the dining room would open at noon. Lilla examined the condition of her nails as she waited patiently to be seated for lunch. Polina considered Lilla was not used to waiting for much of anything. In their earlier discussions, the young lady was always on edge and unwilling to let time pass naturally. She also wondered what the status of the relationship between Lilla and Alejandro was. Had there been a vocal argument followed by Lilla storming away in tears while he shrugged her off as no more than another woman he had bedded? Or perhaps the disagreement had been followed by sex. She was sure either was possible in Lilla's world.

Polina smiled at the young woman and the two of them stood awkwardly for a brief moment.

"Waiting... I need a snack." Lilla did not need to explain her actions, but by telling Polina this minor detail, she hoped to stop her from asking more questions.

Polina nodded her understanding. She decided the opportunity existed to dig further into Lilla's situation.

"I'm guessing your mother does not care for your relationship with Alejandro."

Lilla closed her eyes and shook her head before turning to face Polina. "I guess nothing gets past you. Yea, you're right. She thinks I'm some precious little child who she needs to protect twenty-four hours a day." She paused and straightened her clothes.

Polina realized the young woman was wearing a different outfit than during the questioning. Before, she had on a knee-length dress with black tights and a dark top. She had appeared rather conservative and proper. She had changed and was now dressed in a short skirt not intended for winter, no tights or nylons, and a sheer blouse with tiny embroidered roses. The color of the flowers matched the pink sweater hanging loosely around her shoulders.

"Yea, well… I'm not."

Lilla turned to face the restaurant. The tapping of her right foot against the floor echoed throughout the lobby.

Polina seized the opportunity to dig deeper. She might never get another chance to talk with Lilla without her stepmother present.

"You weren't in your room last night, were you?"

Lilla smirked at the insinuation. Perhaps she should spill every detail of her life to this woman. Maybe that would satisfy her thirst for knowledge. Or was it gossip?

"Well, I wasn't screwing Alejandro, if that's what you mean. All he cares about is his stupid-ass book. And, I should tell you, he seems to be bugged out about you. He completely freaked when I told him you were coming to the library to ask questions." She faced Polina. "Do you think he's the killer? Is that why he started acting so weird?" She turned away again and her voice turned vengeful. She spoke openly to herself. "I bet Alejandro did it. He's such an asshole." Lilla became aware of the noise her foot was making and stopped tapping. She shuffled her feet back and forth, considering if she should say anything else. "I, uh, I couldn't sleep, so I went to the pool. It was like two or so in the morning."

Finally, a piece of the puzzle that fits, thought Polina. She realized there was more to Lilla's story than she had originally let on. The question was, how much more?

"Were you alone there... at the pool? Did you come across anyone else?"

Lilla bit her lip as she considered the question. With nothing to lose, she gave in.

"Yea, I saw him. The dead guy. Dan Steel. He was there with some woman."

"His friend? The actress?"

"No. This was a black woman. She was in the dining room last night as well. Killer body and tall as hell—"

A loud crashing sound from inside the restaurant filled the air, interrupting their discussion. Lilla looked toward the restaurant, but Polina wasted no time. She pushed the dining room doors open and walked quickly in. Lilla followed her, perhaps because she was interested in what had happened, but more so because she was excited to see how Polina handled herself.

The two women stood inside the dining room, listening, and looking. Maybe the noise had been nothing more than a routine restaurant accident. They were joined by Crina and Razvan, who had also heard the noise. Lilla was confused to see Polina had her right arm buried under her jacket.

"What was that?" said Crina.

"I bet it's Ilam again. He is always dropping pots and costing me money."

Another crash filled the air. This time, it was accompanied by guttural screaming. The noises had come from the kitchen, that much was clear. While she could not say with certainty, Polina sensed someone calling for help.

"Wait here!" Polina said, motioning to the others.

Polina sprinted across the restaurant to the kitchen. She stopped shy of the swinging doors and reached under her jacket to remove her gun. Calmly, but with obvious experience, Polina cocked the pistol.

Lilla stood frozen with fear while at the same time mesmerized to see Polina stepping into action with a gun. She had never seen anything like this before except in the cinema. If films were any indication, things were about to get violent.

While the sight of the gun surprised Crina, it was Razvan who was shocked.

"What is happening in my hotel? Who is this guest? Why does she carry a gun? Crina! What is this?" He was beside himself with confusion and anger.

Polina moved her head imperceptibly so she could peek through the door's small window. Satisfied there was no obvious threat, she pushed the door open a few centimeters. The pistol, followed by Polina's face, emerged into the kitchen from behind the door like a cat hunting a mouse. No movement was extra and not a sound was made as she crept in and moved deliberately through the room. There was nothing obvious to indicate a struggle, but what did bother her was the complete absence of restaurant workers. *Where are the chef and Otilia?* Polina thought. She stepped over some pots and pans lying scattered on the floor and moved to the far side of the room. Seeing nothing there, she turned to check behind the food prep table. Her eyes were drawn downward to where Toma was sprawled on the white tile.

A pool of deep-red blood was draining from Toma's crumpled body. Where before he had appeared muscular and formidable, he now looked like a hunted animal clinging to the last moments of its life. The kitchen knife Otilia had pushed into the cutting table earlier in the day had been forced to its hilt into Toma's abdomen. Not a professional attack, was the first thought crossing Polina's mind. Something else was buried deep into his chest, but at this precise moment, she was not quite certain what the implement was.

Toma was barely alive and was attempting to breathe through endless amounts of blood erupting from his mouth. His eyes, vast as a full moon and pleading for his life, were focused on Polina.

She knelt down beside the dying man and he reached out to her, grabbing Polina's arm with his blood-covered hand. The crimson oozed from his fingers and ran in rivulets down the sleeve of her jacket, covering her exposed wrist. Toma's attempts to speak were lost in a mixture of blood and spit. He was unable to say anything sensible and only a volcano of ichor continued to bubble from his mouth. Using what little strength he had left, Toma pulled his head up to get closer to Polina, hoping she would understand his plea. Powerless to hold himself erect, his head collapsed back to the floor. His life was ebbing away and Polina understood it was only a matter of seconds before he would be gone. Toma pushed with the last of his will and tilted his head to the side. He looked past Polina to a door at the far end of the kitchen. His gaze moved from the door to her and back to the door again. He repeated this motion once more before his eyes fluttered and rolled back in his head. Toma was dead.

Polina studied the lifeless body. She had seen death many before and this would not be the last. This was, however, the first time she had encountered two seemingly unrelated murders in the same building within hours of each other. While she experienced sorry for the man who only that morning had assisted them in gaining entry to Dan Steel's room, she could see no immediate reason to connect the two deaths. One had been a clean, precise assassination, and this one a mess of blood and anger. She examined Toma's chest where the other weapon had been used. She was surprised to see a thin metal meat thermometer driven deep into his torso. The circular gauge had not yet settled as the thermometer's reading continued to climb upward, indicating the temperature of Toma's corpse.

Crina burst into the kitchen with Razvan. Lilla was right behind them. Within seconds, the three of them found Polina and saw the carnage that was Toma's dead body. Both women screamed in horror simultaneously. Razvan tried to cover his mouth, but he was at a loss and his hand stopped on its journey. He stepped gingerly forward. Despite his strong managerial attitude toward the maintenance worker, his eyes showed he cared deeply about Toma.

"Is he... dead?" Razvan had seen plenty of death in his life, having been forced by the Romanian Dictator Ion Antonescu to serve with Axis forces in the Battle of Stalingrad. It was only when he learned Romanian troops were persecuting and killing Romanian Jews that Razvan deserted and sided with a small partisan resistance group. After the war, he was able to secure a forged identity and lived under the new name ever since.

Polina nodded to Razvan, acknowledging Toma's death. She turned her attention to Crina. Her scream had become no more than a whimper as she and Lilla held each other close. Polina pointed at the door Toma had been drawing her gaze to.

"What is behind that door?" She hoped Crina would understand the need for a response as quiet as the question she had asked.

Crina was in shock. This day had been too much for her.

"You have a gun?"

Polina put a finger, dripping with Toma's blood, in front of her mouth. *Why are civilians so stupid at times?* she thought.

"Shh."

Crina finally grasped the gravity of the situation and lowered her voice to an almost inaudible level.

"That's a dry storage area. For food… we keep food there. The restaurant deliveries also come in there. There's another door leading to the back of the hotel."

Polina indicated Razvan, Crina, and Lilla should quietly leave the room. Only after the door had finished swinging shut behind them did Polina stand. She found a towel already soiled with kitchen debris and wiped Toma's blood from her hand. She grasped her gun firmly and made her way to the closed door at the back of the kitchen.

Before opening the door, Polina perceived there was blood on the handle and bloody footprints on the floor. Whoever killed Toma had gone through this door and into the next room. *Even an amateur sleuth could follow this trail of breadcrumbs,* she thought. Using the same towel, Polina grasped the handle and pushed down on its lever to open the door.

The room was pitch dark with the only light coming from the kitchen behind Polina. The situation was not ideal since the backlighting painted her in profile but did almost nothing to illuminate the room in front of her. Polina took two steps into the room and stood silent, letting her eyes adjust to the darkness ahead of her. As the room gradually came into existence, Polina could see shelves filled with voluminous cans of food and several huge bags, which she presumed were flour and sugar, or perhaps rice.

In addition to the numerous cooking utensils hanging in the kitchen, this room had many more pots, pans, serving spoons, and other miscellaneous implements she understood were needed in an industrial food prep space. At the far end of the room was an oversized door which, she decided, must be where the food was delivered. On the other side of the door would be a driveway to accommodate whatever truck or van might need to pull up with its deliveries.

The rustling noise from somewhere behind her alerted Polina she was not alone.

Spinning around, she raised her gun and took on a defensive position ready to fire at anything posing even the slightest threat. This was no longer a case of asking questions first and then acting; Polina was in full-on attack mode and all she needed was the smallest excuse to kill.

In a lightning flash of blurred activity, Polina saw movement coming at her and instinctively fired as the dull red-and-white barrel of a burly fire extinguisher crashed into her head, knocking her to the ground. Her gun slid across the room, burying itself out of quick reach under a set of floor-to-ceiling metal shelves.

Polina struggled to fight back the urge to pass out but as consciousness left her body, she saw the profile of the killer against the bright sun and brilliant snow outside as the back door opened and the murderer escaped. As the door swung closed, so did Polina's eyes.

Simon King

Chapter 11

"Right, get ready. Here she comes."

Everett's voice was the first to enter Polina's conscious. She struggled to understand if she was experiencing a dream or perhaps a voice calling her back from the grave. Darkness drifted into light as the blurry profiles of Crina and Everett pulled into focus.

"Polina, this is Everett. Don't be alarmed, my dear. You've had a bit of a crack on the head. Nothing too pressing."

His voice was more grandfatherly than ever. She was on the floor surrounded by Crina, Everett, and Lilla. Crina held a small, bloodied white towel to Polina's forehead. She attempted to sit up but failed. She tried again. This time, Crina used her free hand to help her. As she pieced the situation together, Polina came to understand she was in the restaurant rather than the backroom or the kitchen. *They must have moved me,* she thought but she couldn't figure out how they had accomplished the task and why.

"Oh my God," said Crina. "You had me so frightened. What happened in there?"

"The ladies called for me when the racket started," said Everett. "I realized right away something was not quite straight."

Polina reached to her forehead and pulled away the towel Crina was holding against the open wound. Blood trickled from a sizable gash. It stung as it leaked into her eye. Polina covered the cut again while she struggled to speak.

"Did you see him?" They were the only words she could lace together. As she spoke, she wondered whose voice she was hearing because whoever was speaking didn't sound like her.

"No. There was no one there when we came in. He must've gone out the delivery door. It was closed but not locked," said Crina. "Did you... did you see him? Who was it?"

Polina thought for a moment, attempting to remember the incident. Nothing.

"No. Everything happened too fast. I think I may have shot him though."

"Yes, I think you hit the bugger. He left a trail of fresh blood going out the back door and into the snow," said Everett. "Small wound, I would say. So, he's still out there."

Polina regained her focus and stood up. Wobbling a bit, Everett helped her to a nearby table where she took a seat. "Let's find her a drink. Something stiff, I would say."

Crina dashed to the small bar, which held the libations for the evening meals. Polina made a mental note that the young hotel manager had actually been quite helpful throughout the day. She would need to remember to thank her before leaving.

Everett took this moment to hand Polina her gun. "It is fortunate you had your trusty Walther. That sidearm has been my go-to for decades. What do you think? The same person who killed Steel?"

"Unlikely."

Everett leaned into Polina to speak without others hearing their professional spy-to-spy conversation. "Quite right. Steel was calculated, planned, accurate. No blood, no fuss. Probably never endured a thing based on what I have been able to discern. This young man, the maintenance lad, not so much. Bit of a mess in the kitchen. Too much passion. Nothing professional about this killing at all. The whole meat thermometer thing, an exotic touch, I suppose, if a bit gruesome."

Polina ran all this through her mind as she nodded in agreement. She had to admit she enjoyed having Everett around to help consider all possibilities. Crina hurried back to where Polina was now sitting. She carried a small shot glass, full to the brim with clear liquid.

Polina marveled she was able to move so quickly without letting a single drop escape from the tiny vessel. Everett accepted the jigger from Crina and took a sip. Satisfied, he placed the drink in Polina's hand, which he held steady.

"Excellent choice, Crina. This will put the snap back in her, I would venture to say."

Polina sniffed the glass, recognizing the drink as vodka, and threw it back in a single, determined, and undeniably Russian move.

Her eyes bulged, and she cringed as her throat momentary tightened. The drink brought back memories of her teen years when she partied a bit too much and poured more than a few liters of nasty yellowish kitchen-made spirit down her throat. She was happy to have those years behind her. She handed Crina the empty glass. "Thanks, Crina. You are a dear. By any chance, do you have a bandage we can put on this mess?"

"Of course. I'll find something." Before leaving, Crina eyed Polina desperately. Polina could see the manager wanted to ask the question tearing at her. "What do we do now? There is a killer somewhere in this hotel. It's all too frightening."

"You're right, we do have a killer on the loose. But please, do not worry."

Surprisingly, this was all Crina needed. Those few words were enough to fill her with a sense of security, and she turned away to find a first-aid kit, but before she had taken more than ten steps, Polina called her back.

"Crina, could you please gather the guests and staff together? The time has come to end this farce. Bring them here to the restaurant."

Everett's face lit up with excitement. "Brilliant! Excellent! We may have had a change of players, but the outcome will not be enjoyed by any of them! Bravo, I say, Polina Tolkunova, Bravo!" Everett turned to the others in the room as if to appear in charge. "Once more unto the breach, dear friends, once more!"

No one understood what the odd British gentleman was demanding, but his words did rattle the room into attention and everyone scattered, taking on various tasks and actions.

Simon King

Chapter 12

The snow had all but stopped and all was quiet as the sun's rays tore through the scattered forest, warming the pine trees and dropping branch-loads of powder on the ground below. The hotel was picture perfect against the backdrop of the magnificent mountains. Toma's earlier work with a shovel had removed most of the snow from the walkway and front steps and only a finely packed layer remained with a thin dusting of fresh flakes covering the flat areas. The only color breaking this whiteness was an unmistakable trail of red droplets, marking the otherwise-white landscape leading up to the hotel's grand entrance.

The same rays melting the snow outside flooded into the restaurant through the towering picture window.

Fine dust particles hovered in the air like a thousand tiny fireflies. Razvan and Otilia worked together to arrange a few tables and chairs into a tight semicircle exactly as Polina had directed them to do. Crina walked back and forth from the bar bringing decanters of water and several glasses, which she placed on each of the tables. Having completed the task, she went to the lobby to find the remaining guests.

Lilla and Márta had already arrived and sat without speaking at one table. Lilla's legs twitched and she chewed on the fingernails of her left hand. Márta was calm and focused as she worked on her crotchet project. Everett and Christian, also sitting in silence, occupied another table. Anne-Marie entered the room and stood awkwardly by herself. She was wearing a floral dress that ended above her knees and a modest set of heels without nylons. A bright blue hat sat askew on her hair which she had somehow bundled into a tight ponytail.

Crina returned to the restaurant with Isabella. The actress was dressed for the occasion in a lace top with a tight skirt hugging her legs that made walking either difficult or sexy depending on one's point of view. Her impossibly high heels did not help the matter.

A moment later, Alejandro stepped into the room and paused. The reluctance at being called to this roomful of strangers was written on his face. He desperately wanted an excuse to escape the meeting. He had not changed his clothes since the day before and still looked the part of a lovelorn Spanish guerrilla, who had been exiled to France after the Spanish Civil War where he took up writing about the quest for love during wartime. With every eye upon him, Alejandro walked across the room and found a place at a table some distance from Lilla and her stepmother. He dropped his satchel on the table and moved the bag so the opening faced him, but he removed nothing.

With everyone seated, all looked to Polina to explain why they had been brought together. She stood alone at the window, lost in her thoughts, and attempting to balance the rather disjointed facts she had been able to gather during the day. The death of Toma had been inconvenient but required almost none of her skill to solve. She would take care of this in no time and move on to the more important matter of Dan Steel. In her mind, the case for who killed the American agent was clear. She did have one or two holes in her theory, but Polina believed the killer would help fill those in.

Nervously wondering if she should interrupt Polina, Crina stood and walked over to her at the window. She decided addressing her in a quiet voice would be best.

"Excuse me, Miss Tolkunova, I have everyone here. I think we should begin." She did not wish to anticipate whatever Polina had in mind, but the sooner this mess was over, the better for the guests and for the hotel.

Polina turned and scanned the gathered group. All in attendance stared at her in anticipation. Márta had returned her crochet work to her purse and Lilla was no longer making a meal of her nails. Alejandro sat perfectly still, as if alone in church during a funeral. Razvan and Otilia were seated next to each other and an empty chair to their left indicated where Crina was sitting. Even Anne-Marie appeared somber and attentive.

"Is this all the staff too? Do we have everyone?"

"All except Sofia, the lady who cleans our rooms. She left several hours ago. Sofia lives in a small village on the other side of the mountains and will not return until quite early tomorrow morning. But yes, this is everyone. Oh, and Ilam, our chef. He's in the walk-in refrigerator gathering food for the evening meal. He'll be here shortly. I told him it was urgent."

"I must ask, how does Sophia go home during a storm as we had? Wouldn't it be easier if she stayed here?" Polina had no reason to suspect the cleaning lady other than perhaps for ransacking her room.

"The rest of the staff does have rooms in the basement area of the hotel, but Sofia has a small child at home. During the day, her mother looks after the little girl, but she prefers to go home to her daughter each day. You may not believe this, but she rides a horse here. In certain regions of Romania, people still rely on horses for daily travel."

"Wow, quite amazing." Polina smiled as she remembered riding on her grandfather's horse-drawn cart. Those were such simple days, and she often longed for the return to a life without boyfriends, lovers, guns, and assignments from Red Square. "Well, let's start and perhaps Ilam will be here soon."

No sooner had she finished her sentence than the doors to the restaurant opened and Ilam entered, walking backward. He nudged the door and it swung closed behind him. Ilam was wearing an oversized jacket and held an outsized box in his gloved hands. Surprised at the size of the gathering, Ilam stood motionless, considering the scene. As he only worked in the kitchen and backrooms of the hotel, he rarely came in contact with the guests.

Not a word was spoken, but everyone watched him with a keen eye. Many must have wondered who he was and whether the contents of the box had some bearing on why they were gathered together. The combined attention of the group made Ilam uncomfortable, and he averted his gaze as he moved with a quickening pace toward the kitchen.

"Ilam, could you join us please?" said Crina. She had already told him his presence was required and now wondered why he had decided to head to the kitchen instead.

He stopped dead in his tracks.

"I, uh… I have the meat from the refrigerator. I told you I needed to bring it for tonight's menu. It is still quite cold. I need to put it in the kitchen to thaw."

"Perhaps that can wait," said Polina. "This will not take long. Please, join us." Her voice was pleasing and informal. She was relying on her training, which had told her how best to speak with people in tense situations so they would do what she wanted to be done.

Ilam again took several more steps toward the kitchen.

"Please, I'm sure the food can thaw here as quickly as in the kitchen."

"I won't be a minute," he said as he continued to cross to the kitchen's doors.

"Ilam!" said Razvan. His voice and sudden command shook the room. Even Polina was surprised at his ability to take charge and make demands. "Now! Put the meat on the table and join us. We are all waiting for you. This meeting is what's important. Everything else can wait." He was stern and confident, like a father telling a child to stop watching cartoons and start their homework.

Realizing he had no choice, Ilam placed the box on a nearby table and dragged his feet as he walked to join the group. He took a chair next to Lilla, keeping his gloves on. Polina made a mental note that he had chosen the seat closest to the door.

Everyone was now in place and waiting for Polina to speak. In fact, no one knew what to expect. Polina positioned herself so she was central to the group, making the distance to each person equal, like spokes on a bicycle wheel. Before saying a word, she examined the semi-circle of people, one-by-one, taking them all in and considering how best to begin.

"Thank you for coming together like this and at short notice. I realize this isn't how you planned to spend your holiday. I must say, I didn't think this is what I would be doing when I came to Razvan's beautiful resort." She winked at the hotel owner and smiled broadly.

Razvan sat a little straighter and his face beamed at the praise Polina offered. He may not always understand everything said to him in English, but these words hit home.

"Yea, you got that right, sister," said Anne-Marie. "What's this all about, anyway?" Despite the more formal clothes, Anne- Marie had lost none of her attitude.

"As you are all aware, one of the guests, Dan Steel, an American, was found dead in his room this morning. The room was locked from the inside, but he did not die of natural causes." Polina waited the appropriate amount of time before finishing. She needed to judge the reactions of the group. "He was murdered."

As she expected, Alejandro was the first to speak up.

"How do you come by that? I mean, sure he's dead and he was in a locked room. That much has been traveling around the hotel all morning. But I was told you found no blood, so how was he killed? Was he poisoned?"

"And how is that possible," said Márta, "if the room was locked from inside? Simply impossible. Did someone have his key?"

"These are all quite valid and acceptable questions in a typical situation. But I'm getting ahead of myself." Polina took a few steps toward Everett. "What most of you are not aware of is we had a second murder a few minutes ago." Polina pointed to where the most recent crime occurred. "It happened in the hotel's kitchen."

Murmurs of shock passed through the group.

"Another murder?" said Anne-Marie. She looked along the tables to where Razvan was sitting. "First, she says you have a wonderful resort and now I find out people are getting killed all over the place. What the hell sort of hotel are you running here?" She stood up and looked at the lineup of guests and workers. "Are we even safe staying here anymore?" Satisfied she had made her point, Anne-Marie sat down.

Polina sidestepped the response. "I assure you; this is highly unusual. More importantly, the two murders are not related. The two victims had no connection with each other and the two killers were also not associated in any way. I can tell you this with absolute certainty."

"Who was the victim?" said Márta. "The new victim, I mean. Another guest? And how was this guy killed?"

Crina believed the first question should have been addressed to her, and she stepped in with the answer. "It was Toma, our maintenance worker." As she said these words, she glanced to where Otilia was seated. The young woman placed a hand against her mouth and pushed back from her table, visibly moved to learn her lover had been killed.

Polina walked along the semicircle of tables methodically, looking at each person as she passed. "The most recent murder is much less complicated than the one which occurred last night. I think we need to address the death of Toma first, so we may then consider the much more complex case of Mr. Steel."

She stopped where Everett and Christian were sitting. Both men looked at her unsure of what to expect next.

"Christian."

The young Brit sat back in his seat and raised his hands with his palms facing upward. He was shocked to discover his name called so clinically.

"What! You think I had—"

"Oh no, I'm sorry. I was hoping you might stand over by the door in case the killer decides to make a run for it." Polina could have been more subtle and sensitive, but she knew what Christian's reaction would be and more importantly, she knew this announcement would put the culprit on alert so they more readily exposed themselves.

As Christian stood and walked to secure the restaurant's doors, the rest of the gathered group erupted in voices of shock and disbelief.

"The killer is here? In this room?" said Lilla. Her eyes grew as she looked at Alejandro. *Was it him? I knew I should never have trusted the son of a bitch,* she thought.

"You know who the killer is? You're certain who killed Toma?" said Otilia as she wiped tears from her cheeks.

Eyes and faces were darting to the right and left as the guests and employees considered who might have done the murder. Each person exchanged glares of distrust toward at least one other in the group.

Christian was now at the door and had adopted a stance, making him appear both impressive and formidable. While he was a fit young man, he did not consider himself a fighter, but he was not about to let on to such information. As a consolation, he was satisfied to understand no one considered him to be Toma's killer.

Seeing his lover standing strong and tall, Everett held up his walking stick and shook the cane with approval at the young man. He was a fine stud and Everett was proud to consider Christian his own.

"Are you sure? How do you know?" said Anne-Marie. For the first time, Polina was sure the confident woman's voice quivered as she spoke.

"Identifying the killer is a simple matter of elimination and deduction. I'm aware of who was in the room with me and I also know something about the person who committed this murder."

Polina walked to where Lilla was sitting. She stopped and looked at the young girl. Lilla was nervous. She typically loved being the center of attention, but this absolutely was not the focus she wanted. Not only did she have to contend with her stepmother's constant questioning of her pastime activities, but now some woman she barely knew wanted to make her the guilty party.

"Why are you looking at me? I was in the kitchen, with you. There is no way—"

"No, I am sorry, Lilla, not you." Without saying another word, Polina's shifted her attention to the man sitting to the young woman's left.

Ilam bolted out of his chair, which crashed to the ground behind him. He stumbled backward a step or two and looked at the group, his eyes darting back and forth from one person to another. Knowing he was trapped, he threw off one glove, lunged forward, and grabbed at Lilla's hair, pulling her violently from her chair with his exposed hand. She screamed as the others reacted in horror. Márta stood and faced Lilla and Ilam but said nothing as she considered the situation. Interestingly, Alejandro distanced himself from the altercation. Both Márta and Polina witnessed his movement. Lilla, had she not been in complete terror, may have been aware of it too.

"Shut up, bitch!" said Ilam. His eyes had blown up like two enormous balloons on the verge of exploding. He struggled to throw off the other glove, which flew through the air and landed on a table in front of where Márta had been sitting. His hand, now exposed, was caked with blood. The gunshot wound still oozed fresh crimson, which fell on the wooden floor with a distinctive plopping sound. Ilam cringed as he pushed the bleeding hand into his jacket pocket. He struggled to remove a switchblade knife, which he cracked open and held tight against Lilla's throat.

Lilla stood motionless and only the quietest of whimpering came from the young Ukrainian girl as tears cascaded down her face. She looked down to see Ilam's hand draining a steady stream of blood on her blouse, making the scene more horrific for her.

"Stay calm, sweetheart. He won't hurt you," said Márta. Polina was aware of an unusual calm tone to her voice. Not what one would expect from the stepmother of a child who has a blade pressed against her soft skin.

"Shut up! All of you, just shut up!" Ilam was at a loss as to what to do next. He was far removed from his comfort zone as he had never killed a man before nor held a woman hostage. He was a chef with a temper and his fury had caught up to him.

Everett was the first to move. In a most practiced way, he rose from his chair with his walking stick in hand. "Steady, lad. Steady. You've already put yourself in a bit of raspberry. Don't make things worse." He crept toward Ilam and Lilla at a pace making others believe he was, in fact, motionless.

Polina inched her hand behind her jacket to reach for her gun.

"Don't even think of it, bitch. I'll slice this little tramp like a bagel."

Polina stopped, cocked her head to the side, and held up her empty hands. She knew Ilam would react when she identified him as the killer, but she had not been prepared for him to take Lilla as a hostage. The situation was changing by the minute and Polina needed a new approach.

Everett was discreetly positioning himself behind Ilam. Out of the corner of her eye, Polina saw Everett's actions and moved to distract Ilam by walking in a direction that took his eyes away from Everett. She had no clue what the old spy was planning, but for reasons she did not understand, she trusted him.

"Ilam, right?" she said. "Let's think this through. I'm sure you had a reason to be angry with Toma, and I am sure you didn't mean to kill him."

The truth soaked in and a flash of emotion showed on Ilam's face. He bit his lip and took a step closer to the table, pushing Lilla ahead of him as he moved. This was advantageous for Polina as the chef's move took Everett out of his peripheral vision.

"He's—" Ilam was losing the small amount of rationality he still possessed. He dropped the switchblade a centimeter or two away from Lilla's neck, but not enough to give the girl any relief. "Is he really dead? Are you saying this to rattle me or did I kill him?"

"Yes, Ilam. Toma is dead. The meat thermometer pretty much sealed the deal."

Everett was now less than a meter away from Ilam. Polina moved again in the opposite direction, drawing Ilam's eyes to his left.

"I didn't want to kill him! He made me so mad! He's always speaking to me like I'm a moron. Always treating me like shit! He's no better than me. He's a maintenance man, for God's sake. I don't understand why…" His voice trailed off as he fought back tears.

Everett lifted his walking stick enough so he could grasp the cane's tapered length in one hand. With the other, he twisted the head of the stick clockwise. Without a noise, the head and the shaft separated. In one swift and well-practiced motion, Everett pulled a slender sword, more like a fencing foil, from the cane's hollow shaft and placed the razor-sharp point dead-center in Ilam's ear. He held the steel steady without advancing the foil further.

"One move lad, and you'll be wearing diapers while a nasty nurse spoon-feeds you for the next thirty years." Everett's voice had become that of a military general who could command the attention of the most jaded recruit.

Ilam was motionless. Not a breath escaped his parched lips.

Everett pushed the sword gently into his ear. No more tickling was needed.

"Ilam, I would listen to Mr. Cook if I were you," said Polina. "Now please, lower the knife."

The chef was dripping in sweat. Lilla was already drenched in Ilam's blood and now his salty perspiration. Earlier the sheer blouse had caressed her curves, but now the diaphanous fabric was pasted tight against her breasts.

"OKAY! OKAY!" said Ilam. He delayed for only a moment before removing the knife from Lilla's throat.

"Steady, lad," said Everett. "I do not want to hurt you, but I will if you do anything stupid."

Ilam released his grip on Lilla and she rushed into Márta's arms, crying. Márta held her tight and Polina was struck with the thought that perhaps they did share some small amount of love for each other after all. Not wasting any time, Polina reached back and pulled the firearm she had secreted in her skirt. She leveled the gun at Ilam's forehead as she advanced around the table.

Ilam retained the appearance of a statue with Everett's foil still positioned precisely only a few millimeters away from his eardrum. "Christian, come here please," Polina said without taking her focus off of Ilam.

Christian rushed over to where Polina and Everett had Ilam under control.

"Ilam, listen carefully. No one else needs to be hurt," said Polina. "I want you to drop the knife and take several steps backward, away from the table."

The blade hit the floor with a smack and Everett kicked the knife out of Ilam's reach. As instructed, the chef stepped an additional two meters away from the table while Everett monitored his movement with his foil. Everett may not have been a young man, but his hand was as steady as a neurosurgeon's.

"Okay. Now, Mr. Cook, please withdraw your sword."

Everett pulled the sword away from Ilam's ear with the same swift action he had used to put fear into the chef's heart. He did not return the foil to its shaft, but instead held the blade close by his side. Despite his age, Everett's skill with the foil and his steadfast hands made it clear he was not someone to be taken lightly.

"Ilam, please lay down on the floor with your arms extended."

Ilam hesitated. Did he still have a chance to run? Polina had seen too many criminals who, when faced with an ultimatum, made the wrong choice. She raised the temperature enough to convince him otherwise.

"Come on!" Polina said, her voice louder than any of them had witnessed before. "Faster! Down, all the way! On the floor!"

"Do not be a fool," said Everett. "Do what Miss Tolkunova asks."

Ilam whimpered as he bent to his knees and laid down on the floor. As he slid his arms forward, the wound left an unpleasant trail of red across the hardwood.

"I didn't want to kill him, I didn't. It was a mistake!" Ilam burst into tears. "I'm so sorry."

"Christian, please take off your belt and tie Ilam's hands together," said Polina.

Christian followed Polina's direction and Ilam was now less of a threat to everyone.

"Perfect. Okay, let's find him in a chair."

Polina relaxed her gun hand and pushed the weapon back into her skirt. With Christian's help, she pulled Ilam to a standing position and sat him down as Everett stood behind to keep the chair from moving. The once strong and independent Ilam was now reduced to a bloody, sobbing heap of his former self.

"Crina, can you find some rope and some bandages for his hand?" Polina said. "We can't have him bleeding out and making a mess of the floor."

Crina was shaking in fear. She knew Polina was talking to her and was aware of her words but was paralyzed and could not act. Polina came to Crina and put a hand on her shoulder.

"Crina. I know this is difficult, but please, I need your help."

Otilia stepped over to comfort Crina. Although the two women rarely got along, Otilia considered this to be a necessary moment of unity.

"Come on, sweetie, let's go find some rope or something strong to tie this bastard up."

Crina blinked her eyes and came to her senses. She was surprised to see Otilia standing next to her and holding her arm. Still numb, she walked off with Otilia who seemed to have found a strength she had not possessed before.

Polina looked around the room, considering her options. The time had come to move from the situation with Ilam, to exposing the details of Dan Steel's murder and identifying his killer. To accomplish this, she needed Ilam out of the way so he would not have the attention of the others but at the same time, she understood the importance of keeping him secure.

"Let's put Ilam by the window so I can keep an eye on him." *The position would be perfect,* she thought. He was seated behind the guests, but still in Polina's view.

Christian pulled Ilam to his feet and walked him to another chair by the picture window. He had finished positioning Ilam in the chair when the two women returned. Crina carried some blue towels from the pool while Otilia had a length of sisal rope held in a bundle with a bit of wire.

"This is all we could find. Is this okay?" said Otilia.

"Perfect. Please give the rope to Christian. Once Ilam is securely tied, Crina, can you bandage his hand please?"

Crina had found her strength again while out of the room. She was a different woman now, full of vigor married with anger. This man, who she had, for months, laughed and drank wine with, was responsible for the murder of a man she had spent intimate nights with. She understood Polina's request and would do what was necessary but beyond that, she had no room for sympathy toward Ilam.

Otilia gave the rope to Christian who proceeded to tie Ilam's feet and upper body to the chair as Crina waited with the towels. Deep down she had decided the only reason not to let him die of blood loss would be the crimson stain his bleeding would leave on the restaurant floor.

"Now what?" said Anne-Marie. "What are you going to do with this guy?"

"I'm sure Razvan can summon the police somehow, and Ilam will be their problem. Christian, will you please keep an eye on Ilam? We do not need any further distractions for this next discussion."

Christian pulled up a chair and sat behind Ilam. Everett walked to the young man and patted him on the back before pushing his foil back into the shaft. He smiled as a father would when his son had scored his first goal at football before taking a seat at one of the tables.

Polina positioned herself again in front of the group. She took a deep breath and looked at the nervous people facing her. She had made her mind up about Dan Steel's killer and now was the time to expose them.

"Okay, that excitement is over, so let's move on. We must now address the other problem, the real reason I have asked Crina to bring you here. We need to deal with the mysterious death of Dan Steel in the middle of the night in his locked and bolted room."

Crina finished bandaging Ilam and used one of the towels to wipe his blood from her hands before sitting next to Lilla and comforting her.

"Excellent," said Everett. "Yes, no more of this bother. Brass tacks and all." Both Anne-Marie and Alejandro considered his words but decided they must have been something only old British people said.

Polina moved to the nearest table and poured herself a glass of water. She drank the liquid in one nonstop movement and held the empty glass for a moment as she collected her thoughts and planned her gambit. Her process must be precise and effective, for she wanted the killer to expose themselves to the others.

"So, now you're going to amaze us again with your detective abilities?" said Anne-Marie. This was a halfhearted sarcastic jab at Polina because, in reality, Anne-Marie had been impressed with how she handled Ilam.

Polina ignored her. She had no time to waste on silly retorts and comments. "As some of you may be aware, I am not a policewoman but I have been trained in, among other skills, forensics. Whenever we must examine a crime scene, we have several obvious questions requiring answers."

Polina placed her empty glass back on the table. The vessel wobbled for a second, looking as if it might tip over before finally settling.

"First," Polina said, "who is the victim? Well, we know that, right? Dan Steel. He was a talent agent from America." She glanced at Everett. "This is what he told people, so we shall leave it at that."

"Wait," said Isabella. "Are you saying he wasn't an agent? Damn! That explains so much!" She shook her head while a thousand thoughts crowded her brain.

Polina did not wish to entertain Isabella's comment. She would find time to answer her questions later. "Our next question: where was the victim killed? Again, common knowledge at this point: he was murdered in his room. However, as I already said, his room was locked from the inside with no obvious signs of violence. Strange circumstances, to say the least."

Polina walked to the far end of the gathered tables and turned on her toes dramatically. She paused for a moment before moving along the group of people one slow step at a time. "Dan was killed last night at three-thirty in the morning when many of us were fast asleep. Another fact known by all. But this leaves us with tricky questions. The ones still awaiting answers. These include: how was he killed? How did the killer enter and leave his room if the door was locked? Why was Steel killed? And of greater importance..." Polina stopped and was silent as she let her eyes settle momentarily on each person in the room. Her stare was met with awkward squirms and eyes cast elsewhere. "Who killed Dan Steel?"

"So," said Alejandro, "do you know all these answers? You figured out who killed this guy and why?" His voice wavered as he asked the questions. When he finished speaking, he pulled his satchel close before brushing his hair out of his face.

Polina stepped over to where Alejandro was seated. "Yes, I do. But, let us address the most interesting question first: How was he killed?"

Polina left Alejandro and walked to Anne-Marie where she stopped again. "Only the killer and I know this, but Dan Steel was murdered instantly and bloodlessly by a long, thin object pushed deep into his brain." Polina placed a finger to her head, indicating the point of entry. "Exactly here, behind his right ear. The weapon left only a tiny puncture wound. Almost unnoticeable to the naked eye." Polina continued along the line of seated guests. This time, stopping directly in front of Márta without looking at her.

"What was the weapon?" said Márta.

An appearance of excited interest came to Polina as she spun to face Márta. She moved toward her and leaned on the table.

"Excellent question, Márta! Let's see, what do we know?" Polina bolted upright but did not move away from her position at the table. All the pieces gelled together in her mind and as she spoke and the puzzle became even more tightly joined forming an unbreakable solid. No going back now, she knew exactly what to say and how best to present her case in order to let the killer fall into her trap. "First, the weapon must be thin to leave only a tiny hole in his neck and this device must be long enough to reach the brain stem. The dead man in the other room, Toma, had a long, thin screwdriver which he used when I asked him to find a way into Dan's room. I also found a long, thin meat thermometer in the kitchen capable of doing the job. In a rather gruesome twist, this device is now buried deep in Toma's chest."

Several of the people gathered at the table winced in disgust as they imagined the scene painted by Polina. Otilia closed her eyes and crossed herself. Others, perhaps hiding their unwillingness to appear moved, simply stared straight ahead and sat motionlessly.

Otilia opened her eyes and wiped a tear from her cheek. "So, am I right? Toma killed Dan Steel and Ilam knew this, so he confronted him, and Ilam killed Toma. Right? But why did Toma kill the Steel guy? I don't understand."

At the window, Ilam struggled with his bindings and bounced his chair to face the group. They were all aware of his movement and turned to make sure they were safe from the murderer. Ilam's tears had stopped as he had discovered he, too, was interested in the scenario Polina was presenting about Steel's murder. He knew he would be rotting in a prison for many years, but he wanted to understand the truth about Dan Steel's killer before he was locked away. He also did not want to be involved in a crime he knew nothing about.

"You're full of shit, Otilia! Sure, Toma could be an asshole at times, but he'd never kill anyone. You're so stupid!"

"And you are absolute crap in bed!" Otilia was immediately repulsed by her outburst. She was speaking nothing but anger, for, in reality, she had enjoyed how attentive Ilam had been in the bedroom.

Polina saw the conversation veering in the wrong direction. She needed to remain at the helm if she wanted to make her case effectively. She moved to where Otilia was sitting. "Please, let us stay focused. Your hypothesis is excellent on the surface but as you said, why would Toma wish to kill a hotel guest who was a perfect stranger to him? I may return to your thoughts later, but for now, let's consider the other possibilities."

Polina stepped to the right and positioned herself in front of Alejandro. She looked at his leather satchel resting on the table.

"As I said, something thin. Like a needle."

Alejandro scoffed at the suggestion. But his indignance did not stop him from fidgeting in his chair nervously. He had seen first-hand people sent to prison by his government for crimes they had not committed. Spanish leaders and police had a long tradition of solving criminal cases quickly by simply identifying someone the government did not like—someone whose political voice was in opposition to the stated norm—and lock them up in a hell far worse than even Dante could imagine. Facts were of little importance in cases such like these and

Alejandro knew he must act forcefully if he was to avoid a similar fate.

"Yea, I have a needle. So what? I have diabetes. Bet you didn't figure that out, did you? Alejandro reached into his satchel, removed the vial of medicine and a small metal case, and shoved them across the table toward Polina. "Here! Yea, so what? So I need to inject myself several times a day. Do you think putting a needle in my stomach is something I enjoy? I didn't kill the guy! Why would I? What would be my motive?"

Polina did not answer but instead looked at Anne-Marie.

"And you, Miss Anne-Marie Paris, you mentioned that, not only do you use needles to draw blood. You're a phlebotomist, correct?" Polina looked at each of the others gathered before her. "Such an interesting word. I will be honest, I wasn't sure what exactly the profession was, but Anne-Marie informed me. Anyway, what is more fascinating, is you claim you are in this country to teach a class on how to use"—Polina drew her words out for effect— "long, thin needles to do muscle biopsies. You indicated a needle of"—Polina held up her fingers to indicate the needle's length to the group— "perhaps twenty centimeters, or even more. What do you think, long enough to reach the brain? I think so."

"I help people. I don't kill them. You're making baseless accusations. I would think someone with your training would be more careful about the words you use and the presumptions you make." Anne-Marie narrowed her eyes and crossed her arms.

"Oh no, I have accused no one," said Polina, adding at the last moment, "yet."

Polina moved again, this time stopping in front of Márta. The Hungarian woman was calm on the surface but Polina never considered people at face value. Inside, she sensed Lilla's stepmother was not the caring woman she now pretended to be as she hugged the still-frightened girl.

"I don't use needles. Why are you looking at me?" Her words carried an equal mix of confusion and anger.

Polina studied Márta for a brief second before lowering her gaze to the woman's purse. "Would you be so kind as to open your purse?"

Márta moved in her chair almost imperceptibly. No one else in the gathering realized her discomfort, but Polina did. She watched as Márta's cheek muscles tensed and the fingers of her right hand, which rested at her purse, twitched. Márta was not comfortable with the idea of displaying her belongings to the gathered group, but Polina had put her on the spot. She studied the guests and hotel employees and smiled. With all eyes on her, Márta opened her purse and turned the bag toward her questioning adversary. Polina pulled the purse close and peered inside before she reached in and removed Márta's crochet project.

Márta laughed. Almost imperceptibly at first and then loud enough to startle the group. The others leaned over to see what Polina was holding. Confusion grew on each of their faces as they realized exactly what was in Polina's hands.

"Are you being serious? That is a crochet needle. I like to crotchet, I explained this. The work relaxes me."

"Yes, true. You did tell me. But I think we can all see this needle is thin and definitely long enough to..." She paused briefly while she held up the crochet needle for all to see. "In the case of Dan Steel, kill."

Lilla wasted no time in responding to this bizarre accusation. She pulled away from her stepmother and stood, slamming her hands on the table in front of her. The blood on her hands was not yet dry and they left perfect impressions on the flat surface.

"Look, you're really digging to the bottom thinking my stepmom would kill someone with her crotchet needle. This is ridiculous." She raised a hand and pointed to Alejandro. "Like this guy said, what is her motive to murder some man she has never met? Come on, explain that!" Lilla felt self-conscious about referencing Alejandro in such a public and demanding manner. She glanced at her hands and examined her blouse. Lilla wanted to lock herself in her room and sit in the bath crying for the rest of the day. She had to make do with sitting back down in her chair and attempting to disappear and be forgotten.

Polina returned the crotchet project to Márta's purse and pushed the bag back across the table to the Hungarian. With a smile on her face, she stepped away from the table and pointed a finger at Lilla.

"Exactly! Motive! Why would Márta—or for that matter, anyone here—want Dan Steel dead? Why kill a man they didn't know and had never met before? I will admit, this detail has nagged me the most as I considered all the facts. Why assassinate Dan Steel? What is to be gained? What is being covered up?"

Polina moved to where Isabella was sitting. The smile on the actress's face showed to the group she was enjoying Polina's technique of storytelling. Polina's words were, for her, like a well-written film script, and she had a major role to play. Perhaps she would find was an upside to her agent's death after all. The Hollywood trade publications would absolutely run a story on the incident and her name would be brought up. She would be considered to be relevant once more and maybe a new breed of producer or director would see her as a hot commodity. Her star would once again be on the rise.

"Let's consider the motive. First, Isabella Manson, the unhappy actress who blames her agent, Dan Steel, for her fading career. In addition, she had to always push back on his unwanted sexual advances. Are those reasons to kill the man responsible for making or breaking her calling?"

Isabella's pleasant thoughts instantly turned to shock upon hearing her private life exposed to the others. For her, this was worse than a random shot by a paparazzo while she was on the beach adjusting her swimsuit; this seemed like a personal attack in front of a small group of people. She wanted to scream but knew doing so would only attract more attention. Instead, she sat and boiled internally.

Polina had said all she needed to about Isabella. She gave the actress a wink and continued to walk among the guests and workers, stopping at Everett.

"Or perhaps Everett Cook, the mysterious guest from England with his young holiday companion, Christian Caine. Everett told me he had encountered Mister Steel before, although he would not specify what type of meetings they were. And while I will respect most of his pronouncements made to me in private conversations, I think we all agree it is odd he has so much information about the victim. But do Everett or Christian have a motive? Do either of them have reason to kill Steel?"

Everett's fingers gripped his walking stick with determination but maintained his composure. He also did not like his name being dragged through the mud, but he was willing to give Polina a little wiggle room as he understood acting this way was often necessary to flush out the one you really want.

Christian, too, felt uncomfortable at the indirect accusations. After all, had Polina not called on him to help with Ilam?

"I think not," said Polina.

Polina now stood in front of Crina and Razvan. "Let us not forget our delightful hotelier, Mister Razvan Petrescu. He appears to be completely lacking in a motive for the murder as does the lovely Crina Butaciu, the hotel's manager who is always ready and eager to help any guest in need. Between them, they have made sure our stays at the Teleki Hotel have been comfortable and memorable. But remember, both Crina and Razvan know plenty of personal information about each of us and clearly both have access to the rooms which none of their guests would have. However, while having the ability to move throughout the resort undetected is a useful asset, in the case of Dan Steel neither of them appears to have a motive. We must always return to the damn motive."

Razvan was confused as he was barely following the proceedings, but he could tell whatever Polina was talking about, her words pleased none of his guests. His attention turned to Crina for guidance. She placed her hand on Razvan's arm to comfort him while at the same time burning a hole into Polina with her eyes. She had bent over backward to help Polina from the moment she had arrived at the hotel. With today's multiple tragic events Crina had defended her with every guest only to have Polina now treat her as a possible suspect. Did the woman not understand she had seen her friend and part-time lover murdered only thirty minutes earlier? For Crina, Dan Steel was another guest. He had checked in and would eventually leave. Beyond this, he was no one to her.

Polina left them and advanced to the restaurant's only remaining employee. "Otilia Sava. We all love Otilia for the wonderful treats and drinks she brings to us. The woman who was devastated to learn her lover, Ilam, was responsible for the death of her friend, Toma, actually hides resentment for each of us. Perhaps her attitude is not obvious to you, but she is angered by the hotel guests who are wealthier than her and who travel so freely while she is stuck in a job she clearly hates. But is anger at the size of her tips or the demands of hotel guests a motive to murder one of us?"

Otilia shook her head at every word slipping from Polina's mouth. Her eyes had become narrow slits and her lips pursed with despise she had not felt before toward anyone. If anything, Otilia felt vindicated to feel angry at people like Polina.

"And what about Anne-Marie Paris? A medical professional who was on her way to Bucharest, but decided a night at the hotel seemed like an excellent idea. No one could argue with her decision, right? After all, her stay here did allow Miss Paris to meet Dan Steel in the middle of the night at the pool where an entire bottle of vodka was consumed. All this mere hours before his murder. Perhaps something happened after the poolside meeting causing her to feel hatred toward Dan Steel and made her want him dead. And we have the writer from Spain, Mr. Alejandro Serrat. The way his name rolls off your tongue, so wonderful and exotic! Again, like so many of you, Alejandro appears to lack the motive to kill a hotel guest, but he is also reluctant to answer any of the simple questions I put to him. Each question is met with anger. He even lied to me about what he was doing during the time of the murder. But let's move on."

Alejandro pulled his satchel close to him and Polina thought for a moment he was going to make some sort of loud objection and attempt to leave, but he held his ground. Anne-Marie had remained cool throughout. Nothing seems to bother her, thought Polina.

Polina had now come to the end of the row of guests and workers and stood opposite Lilla and Márta. Everyone waited with a sense of guilt to catch Polina exposing the dirty laundry of the promiscuous young woman and her crotchet-hooking stepmother. But if the killer were not one of them, then what? Would the accusations and slander ever end?

"Perhaps the young, attractive, and... sexually ambitious Lilla Karády is the one we want. Remember, she's not ashamed to seek out the affections of older men whether her stepmother is looking or not. We know she and Alejandro had become quite close during their brief stay here. But perhaps Alejandro had not been enough for her salacious appetite, and she went after Dan Steel in the middle of the night only to have the quick and sordid affair go terribly wrong."

Lilla bolted upright. She was a mess of seething anger and semi-dried blood. Why did everyone instantly think she was a slut? Her father had never objected to the men she dated, and she had always acted with a modicum of discretion, unlike some of her girlfriends who jumped from bed to bed, bringing with them an endless series of doctor visits requiring antibiotics to make them healthy again.

"You are horrid!"

"Disgusting woman!" said Márta. "You know nothing!" Márta reached out to Lilla and brought her back to her seat.

Outside, a dark cloud passed in front of the sun for the light from the window dimmed to a dull gray and the entire room took on a more somber tone. Everyone sensed something was about to happen, but no one could guess what that might be.

Polina moved to the right, her feet making more of an adjustment than an actual step, but the repositioning put her directly in front of Márta. She did not look at Márta, preferring instead to stare back across the others as she continued her presentation.

"Horrid? Yes, perhaps. Disgusting? Without a doubt. But as to whether I know nothing… well, let me explain that each of the hotel's guests and every one of Razvan's employees has vehemently denied killing Mr. Steel. Everyone, except…" Polina adjusted her stare and focused it with pinpoint accuracy, "you, Márta Karády."

The buzz of a single fly filled the room, amplified beyond all reason. The group now shifted in their respective chairs to look at Márta. They all waited with breath held tight for what would happen next.

"All right," said Márta. "Explain why would I kill a man I never met with, I might add, a crochet needle, of all things? And how would I know how to murder him in the manner you describe? Let us not forget in all your walking back-and-forth and insulting each of us with the tiny amount of information you have struggled to gather, you have left out one important detail that you have not bothered to explain at all. Am I right, folks? After all, Polina Tolkunova, you have not told us how anyone might have killed this man if he was in a locked room?"

Márta sat back in her chair, pleased with the series of questions she had thrown at her Russian nemesis. The smugness on her face was unmistakable as though she had shut down a playground bully by taking him out with a robust throw during a vicious game of dodgeball. In her mind, Polina's show was becoming rather tiresome. Márta wondered if she should point out Polina might be using this gathering to take attention away from herself and, in fact, she was the true killer.

Polina nodded her head several times, perhaps accepting she had been beaten in the back-and-forth verbal match with Márta. Quietly, her attitude changed, and she smiled a broad smile that parted her lips enough to allow her gloss-white perfect teeth to show. She positioned a chair directly opposite Márta. Polina then did something no one in the room was prepared for, she retrieved her pistol from the back of her skirt, sat comfortably in the chair, and placed the firearm on the table. One hand was wrapped firmly around the pistol's handle and with a movement meant to garner attention, she clicked the safety into the off position.

"Those are all excellent questions, Márta. Let me now answer them in reverse order."

"So, she's the murderer? This lady killed this Dan Steel guy?" said Alejandro. "If you realized this, then why the hell are we all here?"

"Shut up, you idiot!" said Lilla. Polina took note that Lilla possessed a volatile streak. Earlier in the day, she was ready to drown her stepmother and have

Alejandro's baby, but now she was working hard to protect her.

"Enough you two! You're not contributing anything!" said Márta. She collected herself and prepared for battle. "Okay, now... go on, Miss Tolkunova. I look forward to making an idiot out of you."

"Well, we shall see, I suppose."

Polina relaxed her gun hand and let go of the weapon entirely. She placed her hands in her lap out of view. This was another unexpected move and while some leaned in closer to have a better view of the match of wits, others grew apprehensive and wanted out of the room before the war went terribly wrong. No one wanted to be the next victim, even if only by accident. The one person who failed to look at the unattended gun was Márta; she focused one hundred percent of her attention on Polina.

"The question of how the killer was able to leave Dan Steel in a locked room has troubled me from the beginning. When I examined the deceased's room, I was interested to discover that, not only was Steel's room lacking a finished peephole, with only a rough hole left in the door, I discovered something far more interesting. As I looked at the half-finished hole closely, I discovered traces of what appeared to be dental floss. Moments later, I discovered a container of floss in the trash receptacle at the top of the stairs. This was indeed an interesting development since Dan's room was missing this odd, but much appreciated, amenity. I don't know about the rest of you, but I don't think I have ever stayed in a hotel that provided dental floss in a guest's bathroom. Thank you, Razvan."

The owner of the Teleki grinned broadly at hearing his name. He was sure Polina had said something pleasant, and he welcomed this brief break from the otherwise tension-filled affair.

"But, let me continue. The killer took advantage of Toma's unfinished work to thread dental floss around the door's security device and pass the string through this small opening. This allowed the killer to close the door and pull the lock into place from outside the room. Thus, giving the appearance of Dan having locked the door himself. With no one wandering through the hall during the night, they pulled the floss through the door and disposed of the string along with its container in the trash. Dan was dead in his locked-from-the-inside hotel room. When his body was discovered later, investigators would presume he had fallen in his drunken state and hit his head, causing death."

Márta sat silent. Everyone else, except for Lilla, was visibly considering the circumstances and imagining the dental floss scenario as their combined suspicions grew. Each was beginning to feel like an amateur Sherlock Holmes.

"Now, to the question as to how would you know how to kill someone with a knitting needle—"

"Crochet," Márta said. "I believe you mean a crotchet needle."

Lilla was shocked Márta didn't deny the accusation and instead was more concerned with the type of needles she used.

"Wait, so you're the murderer? You killed this Steel dude?"

Polina did not want Lilla derailing her explanation. Her conversation was no longer for the entire group; she was now speaking only to Márta.

"You are quite correct, a crotchet needle. My apologies, accuracy is essential. I made a mistake earlier not knowing everything about each of the guests and this was pointed out to me by someone who apparently has more information than I. That discussion jogged my memory, and I recalled I had seen you, Márta Karády, previously."

"I assure you, I have never seen you before today," said Márta. "My recall of the people I have come into contact with is perfect. I would remember you and your superior-to-all-others attitude."

"Again, I do apologize, you are correct. We have not met. Not face to face. But I recalled I had seen your face before. I had seen your image in a grainy photograph."

Márta shifted uncomfortably in her seat. No one in the room, other than Polina, noticed the change in position as her movement had been so slight. The body shuffle confirmed Polina was on the right track. All she needed to do was keep pushing and she was sure Márta would expose herself.

"Several years ago, I was sitting in a private reading room in the beautiful Russian Metropolitan Library in Moscow. Have you been had an opportunity to go inside? The building is amazing. You must go some time. Anyway, as I was saying, I sat reviewing countless files, dossiers, and photographs of assets, spies as civilians like those gathered here would call them. Hours and hours, I spent in that building looking at information about all the people the Russian government works with. Some of them are common knowledge and others are more covert. And that,"—Polina moved her body closer to the edge of the table while still keeping her hands in her lap— "is where I met you; in the Russian Metropolitan Library in Moscow. You were staring at me from a black-and-white photograph of Soviet spies. You see, folks, Mrs. Márta Karády is an agent of the Union of Soviet Socialist Republics."

Polina leaned further forward, crowding the space between her and Márta.

"More than that, Márta is a trained assassin." Polina fell back into her chair, creating the maximum distance between her and Márta. "I have seen your work, Comrade Karády. Impressive I suppose, but a bit too gruesome in my opinion." She had her. Check, and mate. "So yes, Márta, you have the skills required to kill Mr. Dan Steel with a crotchet needle."

The room was even more silent than before. If the fly was still in the room, not even his buzzing would have been noticed as everyone sat silently in anticipation.

Márta stared at Polina. Polina returned the stare. This had become an intricate and deadly game of chess, but who would make the next move? Only a second was needed for the decision to be made. Márta lunged across the table, grabbing the gun. She kicked back her chair and standing stiff and prepared, pointed the weapon directly at Polina's face.

"You speak too much!" This was not a trained spy who had eliminated many targets in her long career speaking. Instead, Márta delivered her words through the shrill voice of an angry woman whose deepest unknown had been revealed to the world. A secret she and the KGB had guarded carefully for more than two decades as she traveled the world doing the wetwork her superiors had ordered. She was talented too; some would say the perfect assassin. Her targets were never aware she was coming and the police never considered her a suspect. Every job had been planned to perfection and not a single one was excessive or sloppy. But now she faced a situation she had never dealt with before; she was not a trained killer on a specified assassination assignment, but a suspected criminal standing in front of a group of people with a pistol in her hand.

"Yes, I am a KGB agent, but that is not why I killed that piece of shit!"

Márta cocked the gun, yet Polina remained strangely calm. As had been the case from when she first interviewed her in the hotel's library earlier in the day, Polina was one step ahead of Márta.

"I know," said Polina. "This killing had not been sanctioned by the KGB. You never came here to kill Dan Steel. You had no idea who the man was until last night. I understand you avoided him in the restaurant but only because you did not wish to sit next to Americans who you—thanks to your training—considered to be enemies of the state. No, this killing was… emotional. You were aware young Lilla left her room late last night wearing no more than her tiny bikini. You followed her to the pool where you peeked through the door and caught Steel talking to someone. Whoever he was speaking with, his body obscured any view of the woman. Or perhaps she stood inside the sauna, I cannot exactly address this. What you did know was Steel was drunk and spoke using sexually charged words, making his intentions clear: he was on the prowl for a woman to take back to his room. You were aware your stepdaughter had an attraction to older men so you presumed Dan was propositioning Lilla."

"He's a pervert! She is only a teenager! He deserved to die miserably. I made his death too painless for him!"

"What are you on about?" said Lilla. "I wasn't talking to that old guy. I went to the pool to swim, not to meet him. Yuck!" Lilla was shaking as she spoke. Her whole world and her fragile emotions were collapsing around her.

"Lilla is quite right. While she had gone to the pool, she went to swim, not to meet with anyone. I am sure she was surprised not be alone at such an hour. But no, Dan Steel was not with Lilla, he was meeting with and speaking to someone else. Someone equally attractive but a bit older. Am I correct, Anne-Marie?" Polina had no need to look at Anne-Marie and did not actually expect her to answer the hypothetical.

"Yea. I was there, with him. She was at the pool, too. He was a pretty damn creepy guy. Not my type, man. I'm not cool with old white guys trying to shag me. Yea, we had some drinks. He had brought the bottle so, why not? After a few minutes he starts putting hands on me and telling me he's really into black girls and how we should go back to his room. Uh, no thanks. I left him at the pool like a dirty towel."

Anne-Marie's statement filled in a few blanks in Polina's equation. However, her explanation was not information Polina required at this point since Márta had already admitted her guilt, but later, when the police would finally arrive and Polina would need to speak with them, the phlebotomist's testimony would be helpful.

Polina continued, "Seeing Steel was all Márta Karády needed. She immediately believed he was seducing Lilla, her young stepdaughter. With only this information—or I should say, misinformation—Márta made her mind up to deal with Dan Steel. She hurried back to his room and used her crochet needle to wiggle the lock and gain access to his empty room."

"You're telling me this lady opened someone's door with a sewing needle?" said Alejandro. "Seems like a bit of a stretch."

"Well, of course, I admit that. However, sometime this morning while I was speaking with other guests, Márta did the same thing to my room. I know this because as I found matching scratches in the locks on both Steel's door and my own. I checked other doors and none had any marks on them." Polina cocked her head to the side. "What in the world did you hope to find in my room? Ah, never mind. Not important. Let me continue, you entered the room and locked the door behind you before finding a place to hide, probably the long, thick curtains by the window. If I was in your position, I would secrete myself behind those."

Everyone in the restaurant was following Polina's every word and visualizing the scenario as she spoke. This was easy to do as each room in the hotel had the same layout and the same drapes. Some made a mental note to check if their lock had been tampered with.

"Dan returned a few minutes later. He was still in his wet swimsuit as he threw his room key and towel on the bed and turned to go to the shower. With his back to the window, you took the opportunity and, moving like a leopard, you sneaked up behind him. This was exactly as you had been trained by the KGB and precisely as you had done so many times in the past. Before Steel had a chance to react, you sank your crotchet needle deep into his brain. You understood an area of soft tissue behind the ear was the perfect entry point and once your needle was deep in his brain, a quick twisting motion would turn his brain to mush and guarantee instant death."

Márta smiled and then laughed. Her laughter echoed through the room, making everyone uneasy. All except Polina. She was preparing herself for the final fight.

"Impressive," said Márta. "Your handlers trained you well. As did mine."

Márta straightened her arm, aiming the gun with even more precision between Polina's deep blue eyes. Although Polina's weapon was not one she had used herself, Márta was aware only a single shot would be required from this close a distance. Enough bullets would remain to hold everyone else still while she escaped.

"Yes, they did. The people who trained me taught me everything about investigating killings and tracking down the people responsible. Yours, the people who instructed you, they were less thorough. Perhaps they should not be blamed as you had developed your own killing techniques and your own flamboyant style. Maybe you had no time or interest to learn whatever else they wanted you to understand about methods of killing."

Márta no longer had any reason to listen to Polina. She needed to take action and leave before anyone had the opportunity to follow her. Over the past twenty minutes, she had formed a clear plan in her head. After killing Polina Tolkunova, she would disable the telephone system and steal Polina's car, making sure she put a knife into the tires of any other cars so no one would be able to come after her. Done right, Márta calculated she would be at the Russian border before sunset. The time had come to enact the plan and kill Polina. Márta did not need to gather her nerve as she was always prepared to assassinate a target. Killing was second nature for her, and she would not even close her eyes when the bullet escaped the suppressor. Márta pulled the trigger.

Click. Nothing.

Again, *click.*

"Did you really think I would put a gun loaded with bullets in front of an assassin?" said Polina. She lifted her hands from where they were resting in her lap and let a cascade of shiny brass and steel fall from one hand into the other.

Márta raised the empty weapon in preparation to throw the gun at Polina. As her arm arced forward, it went limp after Everett's walking stick crashed into her head, making a sickening noise akin to someone dropping a ripe melon on a hard surface. Márta's knees crumpled beneath her and she fell to the floor, unconscious.

Satisfied, Everett reached for a napkin and used the cloth to polish the head of his cane.

"Right," he said. "This calls for a stiff drink or two."

Simon King

Chapter 13

The afternoon sun was finally delivering a sense of natural warmth to the hotel lobby as its rays blasted through the monumental windows, making the polished floor shine like a freshly glazed ice rink. At the front desk, Crina was sorting paperwork while Lilla was a mess of tears as she spoke with her father on the phone, which had started working immediately following Polina's revelations about Márta. There were plenty of incoming calls to handle, but before allowing Lilla to use the phone, she had called the police who arrived at the hotel forty-five minutes later. Crina stood in amazement at their speed given the roads must surely still be treacherous, but she did not question their expediency. Instead, she had smiled and breathed a welcome sigh of relief when the approaching sirens filled the air. Razvan stood in the center of the lobby proudly speaking with one of the officers. Everything was in Romanian between them, which seemed to put the hotel owner in an upbeat mood.

Everett sat in a comfortable chair in the corner of the room with both hands resting on the head of his walking stick as he watched with satisfaction four other police officers taking Ilam and Márta out of the building in handcuffs.

Elegant as ever, Polina floated down the stairs with her small suitcase. Although she was actually a short woman and despite the bandage covering the right side of her forehead, she carried herself with a style and confidence usually reserved for runway models. She stepped into the lobby and stopped short as police officers led Ilam and Márta away. A strange mixed emotion of satisfaction and regret filled her. Of course, she was proud for having solved two murders and brought those responsible to justice, but she worried the entire event may have cast a shadow on Razvan's hotel. Perhaps future guests would think twice before making a reservation knowing people had died at the Teleki resort, and in particular, in one of the rooms. Who would want to eat in a restaurant where the chef had killed someone?

"Leaving?" said Everett. "And you were only getting started. Quite a holiday for you, I expect."

He had approached her without even the sound of his walking stick against the stone floor. As Polina looked at him, he became a younger man, a man who was secure in what he was doing for his queen and his country. A man who would move through the world without a care for those who found it necessary to question his sexual mores. Perhaps she had not allowed herself to admit the attraction before, but she liked Everett and hoped to build a bridge of friendship with him. Who knows, maybe he was right and someday political cooperation between the Soviet Union and the United Kingdom might exist. She secretly wished this to be true.

"Not quite what I expected," she said, "but interesting, to be sure. And you? Will you extend your stay? Perhaps a vacation since what you came here for is no longer possible?"

He moved closer to her. Yesterday his nearness would have been awkward, but today his proximity made her feel warm and cared for in a fatherly manner.

"True. My assignment never really had a chance to materialize," he said, "but, on a positive note, coming here allowed me to put a face to a file. Yours. By the way, may I ask… why were you here? I feel your trip to Romania had a purpose beyond spreading disinformation."

She smiled. As always, Everett Cook was right and had more knowledge than he was letting on about. While her assignment did call for meeting Dan Steel, her remit did not include feeding him false propaganda. Quite the opposite. Polina's mission was to ask some pointed questions about American operations and information gathering. She was to learn all she could from

Steel and, when she was certain he was of no more use, Polina was to terminate her contact. The KGB had directed her to assassinate him in his room and make the death look like a suicide. A strange sense of remorse came to her as she realized some in Moscow would feel she failed in her mission. Yes, Dan Steel was dead, but not by her hand. His death—a killing that caused the USSR to lose a valuable assassin, Marta—would be considered a failure by Polina's handler.

"Maybe better if we leave such a discussion for a future time," Polina said. "The topic will make for a fascinating story over a nice bottle of white wine. Perhaps in London?"

Everett smiled broadly. Taking her arm, they walked together to the hotel's entrance.

"To be honest, you actually solved an interesting issue for MI6," said Everett. "We were aware the Soviets had a KGB assassin working in Eastern Europe, and we believed the asset was a woman, but despite our best intelligence, we could not identify her."

Everett held open one of the massive front doors for Polina.

"Always the gentleman."

"And now, thanks to you, we have a name. Márta Karády. And one less nasty to worry about."

Polina stopped on the terrace outside the hotel. The area had been swept clear of snow and the sun felt warm on her face. She thought about Everett's words, wondering where she would fit into a universe of Everett and MI6. She moved close to him, allowing him to breathe in her perfume.

"And what about me? Am I a nasty you need to worry about?"

"My dear Polina. I do not think you are completely aware of who you are yet. You are young with still so much to learn. If you will permit me, I think you are on the wrong side. You have amazing intuition, training, and skills. Considering you as someone who only takes lives is a waste of resources. Seems much too mechanical and routine. You have so much more to offer the world."

Polina marveled at how Everett always seemed to have the right words and said exactly what was needed. Deep down, she had similar feelings about her career and what her lifestyle would mean to her in ten years or even on the next assignment. She was not a sadist; she did not like killing, but she had always operated as directed and rarely if ever, lived with any remorse. But how long could she continue with these tasks? She carried nagging thoughts of what her mother, if she were alive, would think of her daughter. When would the wound come from something different than a fire extinguisher to the forehead, something more permanent?

As they stood on the terraced steps, the doors to the hotel opened and two medical workers carried the body of Toma out on a stretcher. A white sheet saturated in places with crimson blood covered his lifeless body. Polina and Everett remained in respectful silence as the men moved past them toward an awaiting ambulance. At the same time, another ambulance with the body of Dan Steel inside was pulling away.

"Never pleasant. Two men dead. One a spy and the other a civilian, but both just... men," said Everett.

"So true. We do not choose our fate, destiny chooses us," said Polina.

They descended the few steps to the parking lot and walked together through the random traces of snow spotting the asphalt. The police had called for a small snowplow which was doing its best to remove the remainder of the storm's debris, making the area safe and drivable.

Arriving at the car, Polina was surprised to discover the vehicle free of snow. The car looked like a cherry atop a milkshake with its bright red paint luxurious against a field of white.

"I trust you don't mind. I put Christian to good use."

"Well, please thank him for me."

Polina opened the driver's side door, leaned the seat forward, and placed her luggage in the back. Everett, despite his personal choices, could not help but realize the perfection of her female form. If only I was forty years younger and liked women, he thought.

Polina finished her task and pulled herself out of the car and back to a standing position near the vehicle's door. She smiled and looked at Everett with deep respect.

"I am not sure how to say this. Well... the people I report to would frown decidedly if they were aware of what I am about to say, but thank you for your help and guidance. We may be on different sides of this strange game we play, but I feel we are friends now." She leaned in and kissed Everett softly on his cheek.

A royal smile beamed across his blushing face. The bright red outline remained where her lips had momentarily been. Polina reached into Everett's chest pocket and removed his pocket square.

"We can't have you going back in with that."

Before she could remove the lipstick, Everett stopped her.

"Let's leave your mark. I am sure the evidence will drive Christian quite batty!"

He held Polina's hand as he looked into her eyes. This was not a look of investigation or distrust, but one of hope.

"And regarding our friendship, I will paraphrase the eloquent Oscar Wilde. Have you read any of his writings?"

"Yes, I am familiar with his work." With a sly smile, she added, "He's no Tolstoy or Pushkin but for an Irishman, he has an acceptable wit."

"Indeed! Well, he said, and I shall butcher this a wee bit to be sure, 'I prefer to forgive my enemies; annoying them to no end.' Appropriate words, don't you think?"

Polina laughed and handed the pocket square back to Everett before climbing into her car. She turned the ignition and the engine roared before settling into a warm purr.

Everett tapped his walking stick gently on the window. She rolled the glass down and leaned her arm on the opening.

"By the way, if you ever wish to play with the right side, give me a call. We could use someone like you fighting communism and standing up for British heritage."

Polina laughed again. Defection was not an idea Polina presently considered, but she instinctively understood his proposal would somehow remain in her mind for months to come.

"I'll take the offer under review. By the way"— she motioned to his walking stick— "the whole sword-in-the-cane thing, bit over the top, don't you think?"

"Call me old fashioned," Everett said.

With that, Polina Tolkunova backed out of her parking space and drove away from the hotel.